DRAGON UNLEASHED

ACCIDENTAL ALCHEMY
BOOK ONE

JESSICA WAYNE
HEATHER HILDENBRAND

Edited by Love Kissed Books

Proofread by Dawn Y

Cover design by Paradise Cover Design

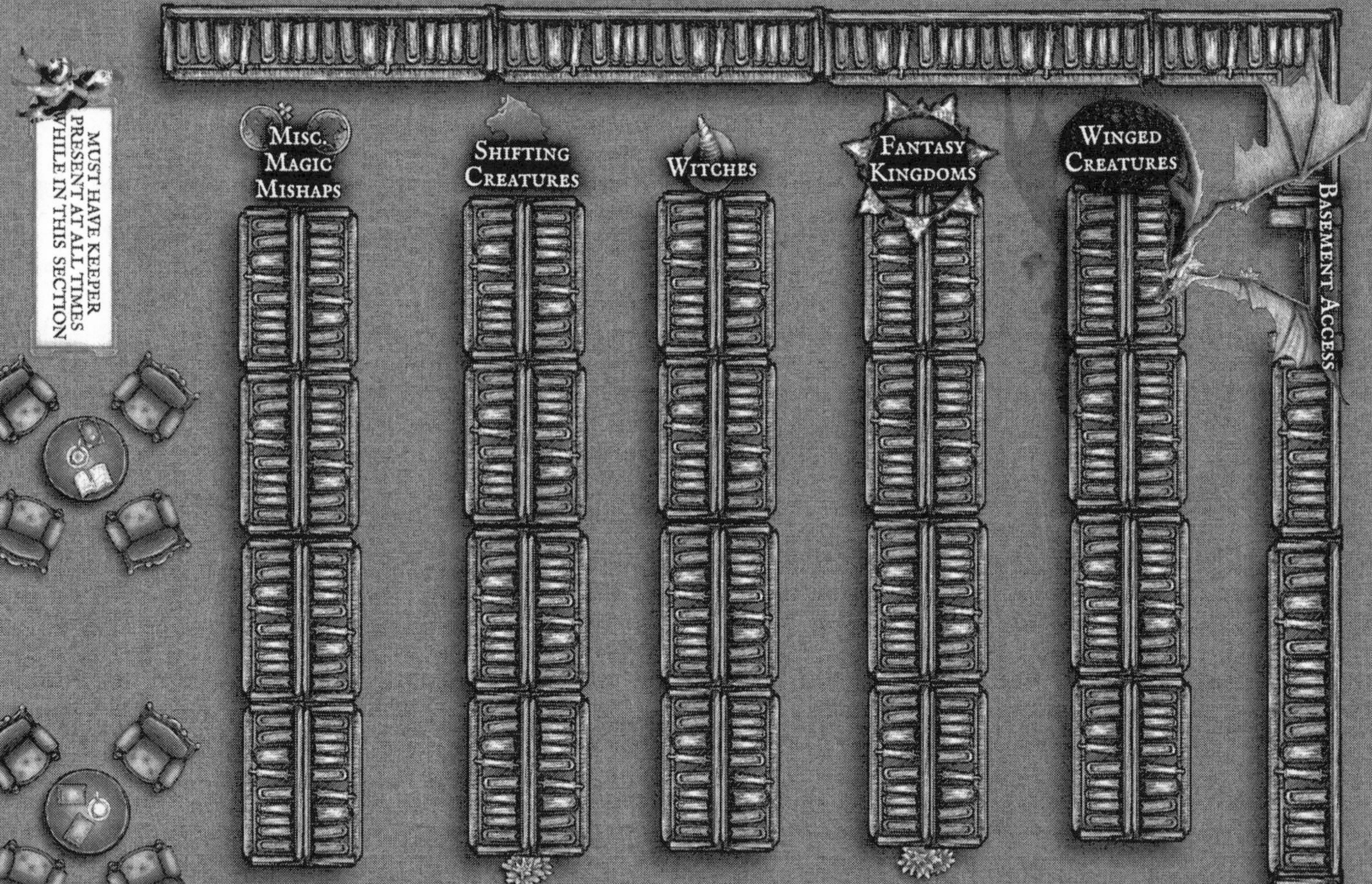

MUST HAVE KEEPER PRESENT AT ALL TIMES WHILE IN THIS SECTION
Misc. Magic Mishaps
Shifting Creatures
Witches
Fantasy Kingdoms
Winged Creatures
Basement Access

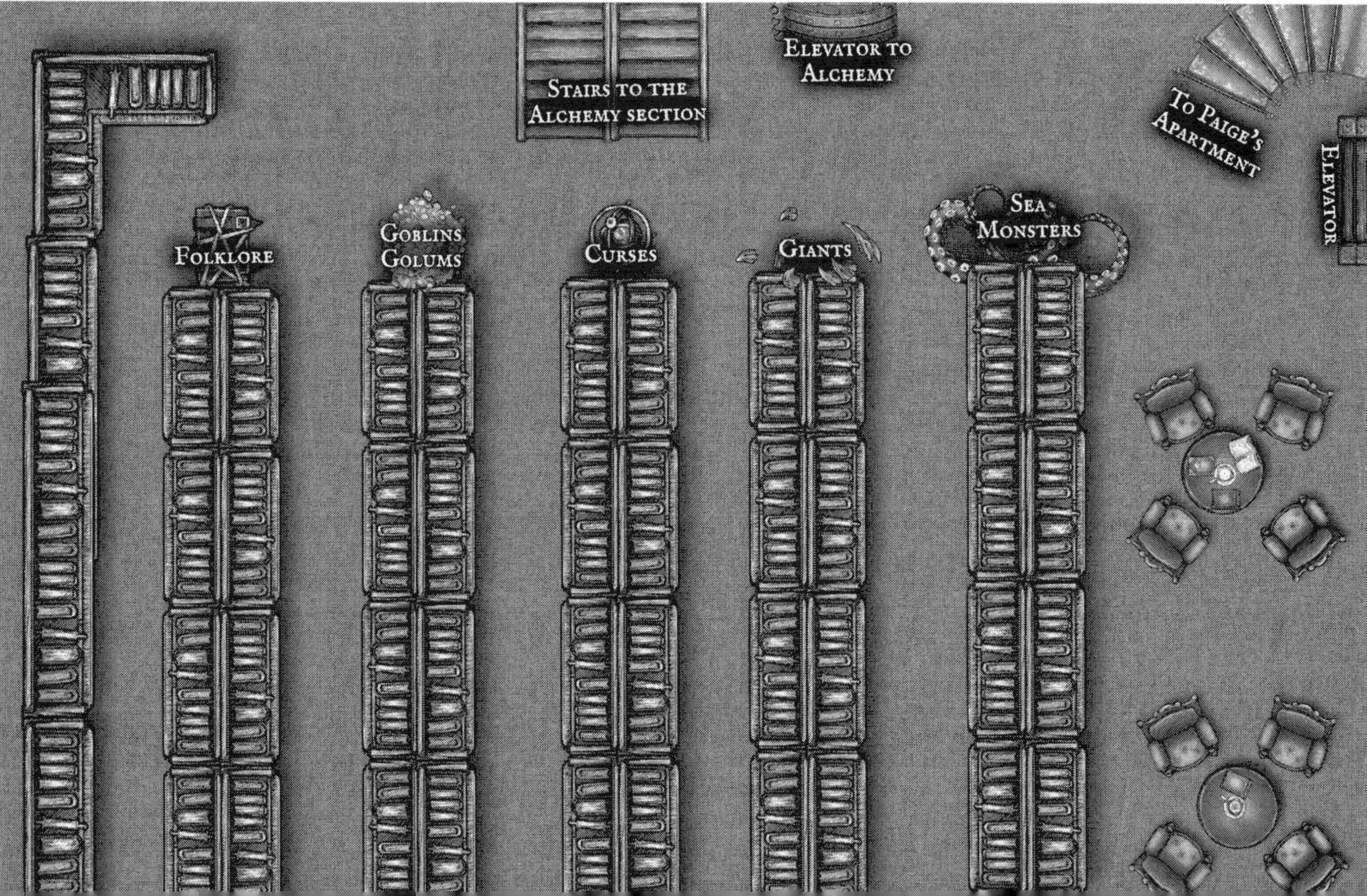

Stairs to the
Alchemy section
Elevator to
Alchemy
To Paige's
Apartment
Elevator
Folklore
Goblins
Golums
Curses
Giants
Sea
Monsters

CHAPTER 1
PAIGE

This particular Thursday starts out like every other. I'm early to rise, quick to coffee, and off to work. The fact that my workplace is the ancient and very secret library that exists one floor below my small Boston apartment is just a bonus that means I don't have to deal with rush hour traffic or, well, humans in general.

Then again, it's not my choice to remain separate from the humans, so I'm not sure that's actually what I'd call a *bonus.* But I've made my peace with it. There is—unfortunately—no other option. The work I do here is too important to risk creating any attachments *out there.*

As an intern for the Athenaeum, the creatures I interact with are few and far between—and rarely ever human. Trolls, giants, elves, fae, shifters—the clientele that come to study or search the library are diverse and strange. Have you ever met a banshee bookworm with a top-secret clearance? It's not a combination one might expect. Also, not to stereotype, but banshees are just weird in general.

With my earbuds streaming a spicy alien romance audiobook, I spend the morning patrolling the ogre section and watching for anything sneaky or out of place among the quiet stacks.

The Athenaeum has one purpose, and that is to contain the threats trapped among the pages of the volumes kept inside it. As the library's newest—and most hopeful—intern, my job is to make sure nothing inside the books contained here makes it out again.

Unfortunately for the Athenaeum, I kind of suck at it.

As if to prove my point, a large tome on the end of the shelf shakes ominously as I pass it. A single, gnarled green finger pries itself from between the pages, attempting to push the book open. I rush forward, adrenaline surging. With two hands, I grab the book and squeeze it shut again.

"Clauseruntque," I hiss and the green finger withdraws as the book seals itself shut at the command of the magic.

Exhaling, I re-shelve the book into its proper place then let go and back away, bumping into the shelf at my back. Several books vibrate with the impact, and I suck in a breath, jumping clear of them before my clumsy ass can do any more damage.

A moment passes, and the books fall silent again.

Damn, that was close.

It happens far more often than I care to admit. As though, for some reason, the books *enjoy* toying with me. Truthfully, I wonder if they can sense how afraid I am of screwing things up. They don't act like this for the full-fledged keepers, that's for sure.

I tune back in to the audiobook still playing in my ears and resume my patrol, fingers crossed the incident wasn't strong enough to raise any alarms with Hoc.

I can't really afford any more fuckups.

Not after I *barely* managed to avoid getting thrown out for the last one.

So, I keep strolling, putting one foot in front of the other while I imagine the hands of a deliciously muscled blue alien running all over my body.

A shifter—as evidenced by her golden gaze—steps into the aisle and looks up. She mouths something, but I can't hear her. She repeats—

" . Sorry!" I pull one of my earbuds out.

"No biggie," she says easily. Her blonde hair is long and braided over her shoulder. When she smiles, I get the sense that she's new to the library. Mainly because the smile doesn't reach her eyes, and it's not hard to sense her uneasiness here. She's not the only one. Most of our guests don't realize how alive this place truly is until they experience it for themselves.

"Can I help you?" I ask.

"Yes. Please. I'm trying to find some history on shifters. Books detailing what comes first in terms of creation. A real chicken or the egg type of situation." She laughs.

I return her humor, deciding that, if I were going to make a friend outside of this place, she could be one of them. "Yes. We have quite a lot of reference material about shifters in the non-fiction section. Unless, of course, you want a spelled fictional story."

"No, thanks," she says with a shudder. "I've had enough dealings with spells to last a lifetime."

"Well—"

"Serenity," she offers.

"Serenity," I continue, "You can find the non-fiction down the hall and toward the back. There's a sign over it, though it might not be lit yet." *Damn gnomes. They had* one *job this morning.*

"Great. Thanks so much—"

"Paige," I say.

"Paige. Great name." She grins, but after so many years of jokes, the humor doesn't hit me in the same way anymore.

"Thanks, it's fitting, I suppose."

"Very. Have a great day!" She waves and turns. Normally, supernaturals are escorted through the more volatile sections of the library. The ones who need keeper or intern status to enter. For what Serenity is looking for, though, she shouldn't run into any issues.

Unless, of course, she tries to break into the restricted areas. But, as far as I know, that's never happened. The library's magic is too strong for that. It sees everything.

I continue my perusal, re-shelving books as needed and checking through the areas to make sure no one has wandered where they shouldn't be, and by the time I surface again, I realize that the entire morning has passed without much incident.

Winning! My stomach growls, and I become aware I've very nearly missed lunch, thanks to my audiobook as a pleasant distraction. The story is about a human woman who crash-lands on an alien planet only to be saved by a large, muscled creature with two dicks. *Two!* Her dream come true.

If only.

I snort, enjoying the spicy scenes and the fiction of it all. Humans write the best fairy tales. This place? It's full of stories that are much too real to be enjoyed.

On my way back to the break room, I reach the witch section. There's a title called Midnight Falls something-or-other, and my fingers brush over the spine as I try to imagine what a place like that would look like. The spine moves beneath my hands, and I jerk away again, scowling at how unsettled it leaves me.

A noise ahead snags my attention. Grunting. And then a heave of breath and a *crack!*

The sound of a weapon wielded has me running toward it.

Rounding the corner, I pull up short. Blossom, a female keeper not much older than me with stark white hair is standing over a body that's currently oozing blackened blood into the carpets. Blossom has a severed troll head clutched in one hand and a blood-tipped axe in the other.

She looks up at me, her sharp gaze mildly annoyed at seeing me here. "He a friend of yours?"

"What happened?" I ask, eyes wide.

"This asshole was shelved incorrectly." Her glare turns accusatory, and I jolt, realizing her meaning.

Interns are the only ones who shelve books. And I'm the only intern. Which makes that exclusively my problem. *Shit.*

"Does Hoc know?" I ask, keeping my voice a near whisper.

Before she can answer, a harsh blaring sounds overhead, and dread spears through me. Double shit.

Blossom gives me an apologetic look. "He does now."

Then she returns her attention to the decapitated troll and mutters a string of words in a language I've yet to learn. The language of the keepers. Magic sparks, engulfing the troll until its body and corresponding head are sucked into the open volume lying at her feet.

Blossom grabs the book and slams it shut with a muttered, "Clauseruntque," to cap it off.

The pages stick.

She hands the book to me.

"At least it wasn't the main character. Come find me when he's done yelling at you," she says, and I know she means Hoc. "You owe me a drink for that one. I got troll-blood on my new shoes."

I look down. Sure enough, bright blue troll blood coats her normally shiny Doc Martens. Great. "Add it to my tab."

TEN MINUTES LATER, I sit with my legs crossed and painted green nails tucked beneath my thighs. It's a childhood posture; a guilty one at that. My unruly blonde hair has fallen into my face, and I make no move to tuck it back again. From the other side of his massive desk, Hoc's deep baritone voice washes over me as he goes on with his lecture, the very sound of his disappointment transporting me back to any one of a million similar lectures I received here as a kid.

At seven years old, it was probably something about not making houses for my Barbies with castles I'd extracted from books. At twelve, I remember being taken to task over talking the gnomes into giving me a flail to train with; a weapon that led to pretty much the full destruction of my bedroom when I tried practicing on my own. To be fair, the gnomes are easily talked into most anything, really. And if they cannot be talked into it, Sour Patch Watermelon candy will do the trick.

At sixteen, Hoc found me trying to flirt with one of the male interns—a wyvern who would have just as soon eaten me as, well, *eaten* me. After that, Hoc had immediately dragged me in for a safe sex talk that thoroughly embarrassed us both.

Today, the *déjà vu* brought on by my current offense is almost comical. Even at twenty-five, I still feel like a kid when Hoc sits me in this chair and takes this particular tone.

I do my best to focus, though. Getting caught daydreaming is worse than actually listening to him drone on. With that in mind, I look away from his nameplate where I've been staring blankly at his name, Hoc Novensile, Head Librarian, and instead refocus on where he sits across the desk.

Like his lectures, Hoc's dark brown beard is timeless, as is the ire in his strong yet weathered gaze. His professor's robe is patched in dozens of places from refusing to replace it with a new one over the years. Even his office looks the same as it has my whole life, with stacks of books littering every bare surface including the floor.

The fact that a troll serves as head librarian to the most revered and dangerous library in the supernatural world still surprises most folks. Not me. Hoc is too perfect for this job. No, he *is* the job.

Overhead, a high ceiling accommodates Hoc's massive frame and considerable stature. Unfortunately, it also allows for his voice to boom even louder from the rafters as he goes on at me about mis-shelving dangerous books.

Separately, most of them cannot open on their own. *Note, most of them.* But, when two volatile tomes are placed together, the magic mixes, and the most recent spell placed over the newly shelved one gets canceled out. Which means, most of the time, it's the seal spell that goes.

"You know better, Paige. That's what I can't understand about all this."

When he pauses, I realize he's waiting for me to say something. "It was an accident," I rush to say. "I must have been lost in the book I was listening to."

The moment the words are out, I know they're the wrong ones. His forehead crinkles, and his mouth tightens as he steps up to his desk and braces his hands, leaning over it to where I sit.

"Getting distracted in the library is dangerous enough. But when you're this close to being taken away from here?" He shakes his head sadly.

I wince.

"One more strike," he says before I can answer. "One more offense and the council will insist you be dismissed from the position of intern. I don't have to tell you what that would mean."

"No," I agree quietly.

I know exactly what that would mean. In fact, the

mere thought of it makes me shudder. He's right. This isn't just a job. And I'm not just an intern either.

Not to mention the council has never liked me. Then again, they don't like anyone. Even with Hoc, they seem to be merely tolerating him.

"But... Hoc, you're the head librarian. Surely you can speak for me. Make them understand. In fact, maybe there's a different role I can move into. Something more suitable for me—"

"The council won't allow me to offer special treatment. You know that. The rules and expectations of the Athenaeum are absolute. Beyond sacred. The council's only duty is to make sure no one is above the laws of this place, and they don't waver. This isn't a favor I can ask or a string I can pull. Not even for my own daughter."

"Maybe I'm just not cut out for the Athenaeum," I say.

He looks horrified, and I can't blame him. "Paige, even if that were true, you know what happens to interns who are dismissed. Your memory will be wiped. You'll be banished." He swallows as if the words are hard to say. "I'll never see you again."

Guilt weighs me down at the anguish in his eyes. Hoc is the only family I have in the world, and I can't let him down, nor am I willing to give him up—even if it means being stuck in a job I don't love. "I'm sorry, Hoc. You're right. I'll do better."

"One more month," he says, his voice strained. "That's all you have left before your internship is complete and you officially become a keeper. Can you just stay focused and keep your head down for another month? For me?"

I take a breath that's meant to steady me and instead find my throat closing around it. "Yes," I manage to tell him.

He relaxes, though not by much. "Good. Shadow Blossom for the rest of the day. She'll keep you out of trouble."

I nod, rising to my feet, ready to get the hell out of this room. But Hoc stops me, rounding the desk to block my path.

He gazes down at me with eyes that are far gentler than one might expect upon first glancing at the giant. "You know I love you, daughter."

I smile. "I know. I love you, too."

He holds out his arms, and I step into them, hugging him until I can feel us both let go of the tension and worry.

"I have faith in you," he says when he pulls away.

"Thank you, Hoc." I leave before he can glimpse the truth in my eyes--that I'm not sure I have faith in myself.

CHAPTER 2
ARIES

"Ha! Your Highness, you'll have to be faster on your feet!" Metal meets metal when my sword clashes with Leo's. Sweat beading on my brow, it takes a good portion of my strength to remain on my feet.

Of course, I'll never admit that. Despite the strain, I grin, happier than I've felt in months. "If I were any faster, my victory would be far too easy to obtain." I whip my blade back then spin and kick his legs out from beneath him. In the blink of an eye, I'm back on my feet, the dull edge of my training blade pressed against his throat. "And don't call me Your Highness, Your Highness."

Leo's cheeks are flushed as he closes his eyes and leans his head back against the soft dirt of our training ring. A ring I don't visit nearly as often lately.

Reaching down, I offer him my hand, and he takes it.

Once my brother is on his feet, he brushes off his riding pants and shakes his head. “You kick my ass every single time, and yet I never seem to learn from it.”

I chuckle. “The day I cease kicking your ass is the day I’m being buried next to our father.” The dark humor is my only way of coping these days. I should have had a few more years at least. Years to find my mate and make my own mark before being forced to take on an entire kingdom.

And yet, here I am. Trapped in the midst of a nightmare.

He clasps my shoulder. My only sibling, Leo is my height, though where I have filled out with muscle, he is far more slender. He claims he’s built for speed whereas I am the brawn.

His bright blue eyes light up as he grins at me. “Let us hope that day is far from today, big brother.”

“Yes, of course. Can’t have you forgoing your trip around the world to step up and take my place on the throne.”

Leo visibly shivers. “Being king is quite literally my worst nightmare.”

I don’t bother mentioning that, unlike Leo, it’s the one thing I’ve lived and breathed for all my life, only because he already knows it. Just as he knows how miserable I’ve been ever since our father died. We’ve both grieved for the man who was more than just a king.

But even before his body had been placed into the ground, the expectations and responsibilities of a future king fell squarely on my shoulders, and my lack of a mate went from subtle disappointment to political nightmare. Without my mate, I am trapped in this hell, unable to fully take the crown until I've found her yet too bogged down by the needs and wants of my constituents to actually go out and look.

Royal purgatory. That is precisely where I will remain until I am able to take my bride.

"You headed inside?" Leo asks, pulling me out of my brooding.

I shake my head and take a swig of my water. The leather is smooth beneath my fingertips as I offer it to my brother. "Going to take to the skies for a while. I need to check the southern borders."

Leo returns my water and grins. "Hiding from Mother?"

"She will not rest until she has found my mate," I tell him with a groan. "And I'm truly beginning to believe it's an impossible venture. She's paraded nearly every eligible maiden in front of me. Weeks of entertaining women I feel absolutely nothing for."

"Your fate is truly horrible," Leo replies, feigning misery by pressing a hand to his heart. "A parade of beautiful women. Sounds positively dreadful."

I glare at my brother. "You go ahead and laugh it up, brother. As soon as she finds my mate, you'll be next."

Leo pales slightly. "Parades of women, I can handle. Our own mother doing the choosing, not so much."

"Aries!"

I stiffen. *So much for taking to the skies.* Turning, I face my mother, the queen, as she comes to a stop beside the edge of the ring. Her dark hair has been braided to the side, the emerald gown she's wearing pristine. The woman never looks disheveled.

Truly, as far back as I can remember, Dorthea Nemos has never had a hair out of place.

As she's told us on many occasions, the Queen of Astronia is expected to be the picture of grace and control. Two qualities she has assured me my future wife will possess. Which is yet another reason finding my mate seems so far-fetched.

I love my mother, but the idea of marrying someone like her is honestly even less appealing than being drenched in troll blood and dropped into a sulfur pit.

Still, it's not seeing her show up here that has me truly annoyed. It's the woman walking beside her. Dressed in a gown the color of spring tulips, her red hair is piled high upon her head and adorned with tiny white flowers. Her face has been painted to the point of pageantry despite the fact that we're hardly at a formal event.

She smiles widely at us, her eyes bright—and assessing. It's that assessment in her gaze that sparks my annoyance. I've seen it a hundred times before. Like she's trying to decide whether her name or mine should go first on the wedding invitation.

"Morning, mother." Leo steps forward first and kisses her noisily on the cheek.

"You missed your appointment." My mother's tone is scalding, her gaze firmly on me. I know exactly what appointment she means, too. A blind date with the woman before me. It had sounded, honestly, worse than the war brewing should I fail to take a mate. So, I came here instead. Though, based on the woman's obvious interest in my brother, she doesn't seem to mind my offense.

"I'm sure Aries had a good reason," the woman coos as she reaches out and brushes dirt off of my brother's arm. "Combat training is such an important part of being king."

My mother winces.

Leo, however, grins back at me. "You have the wrong brother, love," he says then steps aside and gestures to me.

The woman's cheeks flush crimson. "Of course, I was merely cleaning the dirt from your tunic."

"Of course you were." Leo winks then turns to me. "I'm off to train the next generation of Astronia fighters." As soon as he's behind our mother, though, he wiggles his brows at me.

The bastard.

"Very good, darling, see you at dinner," she tells him.

And then with her full attention aimed at me, she asks, "Were you planning on showing up at all?"

The fact that she's willing to ask me this in front of a stranger shows just how angry she is.

"My apologies. I'd planned to be there, and then something came up. A security issue reported early this morning," I admit. "I wanted to fly over and check the southern border. Ensure that the horde remains at bay."

"You have a duty—"

"It's quite all right, Your Majesty," the woman interjects. My mother's eyes widen, but she doesn't correct her for her interruption.

Honestly, if I weren't more than happy to miss the ass-chewing, I might have been offended on my mother's behalf. No one interrupts a queen, or if they do, they haven't met my mother.

"May I have a few moments with Aries?" the woman boldly asks.

"Of course," my mother bows her head graciously then leaves me alone with the woman. So she got her way after all.

"Your Highness," she begins, bowing. When she straightens again, the assessing gleam from earlier is replaced by a coy smile. She inches closer. "My name is Esma Oleander."

"Lovely to meet you, but I really must—"

"It is truly not a problem that you missed our

appointment. In fact, now we have the perfect moment alone to get to know one another better."

I don't bother to hide my grimace.

Interrupting my mother is bad enough, but the woman seems hell-bent on not allowing me to speak either. She loops an arm through mine and guides me toward the gardens. "I know how tiring your responsibilities are, and I, for one, am more than grateful you are training with your blade. Proficiency is far more important than punctuality if you ask me."

I hadn't, but she continues anyway, "What you need is a wife who can help balance your responsibilities. Someone who will be punctual on your behalf so you may tend to—well—the more physically challenging tasks." She stops walking and faces me, not bothering to hide the innuendo in her words.

Surrounded by bright blooms, the woman looks as though she might simply blend into the topiary around us. She's beautiful, there is no question about that. High cheekbones, an angled face, bright eyes—but standing here in her presence, I am lacking the one thing I am desperate for: connection.

"My grandfather's mother was royalty," she explains. "So, our children will have that on my side as well. Three, I think, is a good number for a royal offspring." She grins at me, eyes sparking with interest. "Unless, of course, you'd be interested in more."

"I appreciate your interest, Madame Oleander, but you are not my mate."

She waves her hand as though dismissing me. "Let's be frank with one another, especially if we are to be married." Her assumptions know no limits, I see. "You and I both know your mother is little more than a figurehead." I stiffen at that, but she presses on. "The horde will not wait much longer before they storm our borders. You need a wife to secure your place on the throne and to stave off this war. Not to mention heirs. And with my royal heritage and shifter blood, our union will be more than enough."

"I need a fated mate to ensure the dragon line continues," I remind her.

"Perhaps not," she replies with an unconcerned lift of her shoulder. "My kind can fly as well."

"And what kind is that?" I can sense that she's a bird of some kind, though she's not meek enough to be a sparrow shifter, nor is she fierce enough to be a peacock.

"Flamingo," she tells me as she straightens. "Could you not tell?"

Fucking flamingos. Her bravado makes sense now. Her kind love to flaunt themselves and see no harm in doing so even when that flaunting is done by insulting others. "Of course, it makes sense now," I reply with a tight smile. "I truly apologize, Madame Oleander. You seem like a kind woman, but you are not my mate, and I am unwilling to settle for less."

Her expression cools, and if her forwardness weren't bad enough, in this moment, her pouting reminds me a bit of my mother. "You would risk war for your petty heart?"

My smile turns razor-sharp. "My heart is not your concern. And you'd do well to watch your tone with your future king."

Her gaze narrows, and she points a finger at me. "You are going to be the destruction of this kingdom," she accuses. "All because you cling to some foolish notion that dragons must prevail. Your mother is not a dragon. She is a fae, is she not?"

"She is, but she was my father's true mate." I keep my voice calm, my tone steady, even as the beast inside of me surges to the surface as a direct result to my anger.

"Your brother can continue the line. Your job is to take a queen so she may help protect these lands from the hoard."

"You are vastly overstepping, Madame Oleander," I warn. "And should you continue, I will have you escorted from these grounds. What might your family think then, I wonder?"

She growls—actually growls at me. It's almost impressive really. Especially for a flamingo. "You cannot—"

"Good day," I interrupt then turn on my heel and march out of the gardens. My mother is waiting just outside, inspecting some roses and pretending to have not been eavesdropping.

"Please see to it that Miss Oleander gets home safely," I tell my mother, who, to my surprise, smiles knowingly.

"Of course, son."

"I'm off to check the borders." Without waiting for her to argue, I lean forward and kiss her cheek. "I promise, I will find the one I am destined for."

In a rare show of emotion, my mother sniffles. "I only want what's best for you."

"I know you do." I smile then leave her behind and let my beast free. The moment I'm clear of the arena, my dragon bursts from me, obsidian scales covering my flesh as I grow larger than any other shifter in existence, and two massive, leathery wings spread out on either side of my body.

I shake, the beast within beyond thrilled to be free of the confines of my mortal form. Turning to my mother, I drop my head and snort, my way of letting her know I will be home soon.

Beside her, Miss Oleander stares at me in awe, her eyes so wide they're nearly completely white. Unable to help myself, I shake my head at her then push up from the ground and take to the sky.

Wind whips at my scales, a welcome chill that thrills me beyond measure. Before I'd been bogged down by responsibilities, I'd fly just like this each morning.

Now, I'm lucky to break away twice a week. Since the

moment my father left this world for the next, my every waking moment has been packed full of new responsibilities.

Until I find my mate, the throne eludes me. And Esma was right about one thing. My mother *is* simply a figurehead at this point. Our kingdom doesn't recognize a single ruler; only mated pairs. It's a tradition that has existed for centuries because it spreads power rather than consolidating it to one single ruler. The hoards don't care about that so much as exploiting a weakness. My mother's precarious position as a lone queen is all that stands in the way of an all-out invasion.

It was dragons who'd sent the horde running from these lands centuries ago, and without a dragon on the throne, we're mere moments from total catastrophe.

Swooping low, I fly over our traps, checking to ensure they are empty. I hadn't lied about the disturbing security reports. According to our scouts, there's been zero movement detected in a region where the attacks used to come weekly. The horde has been uncharacteristically quiet as of late, something that makes me even more uneasy with each passing day.

Our borders are at least three days' ride from the castle grounds, but up here, with massive wings propelling me, the trip takes barely more than a couple of hours. Gliding over rocky mountains tipped with snow, I drop down beside a waterfall. Droplets of spray from the falls coat my scales as my talons dig into the soft dirt.

I shift back into human form, using this time alone to get my head right. Choosing a mate is more than a desire; it's my royal responsibility.

I just haven't been lucky enough to find her. *Yet.*

I dive into the water, the coolness enveloping me. Swimming to the bottom, I hold my breath and allow the quiet to calm my racing mind. One day, I will find her. One day, I will be the king my people deserve.

CHAPTER 3
PAIGE

Somehow, I make it through the rest of the week without incident. Well, unless you count Bingo—our predatory hellhound—taking a bite out of a visitor Thursday morning. But I wasn't involved in that particular chaos-party, thank the gods. Friday evening, I breathe an audible sigh of relief when the clock strikes quitting time.

Three more weeks.

I square my shoulders, pep-talking myself about my promise to Hoc. In three weeks, I'll have successfully completed my internship and become a keeper. After that, my tenure here is all but guaranteed. I ignore the little voice whispering in my head that I'm going to hate every minute of it. I'm sure I'll learn to love it, especially considering the alternative is never seeing Hoc again. Rounding the corner toward the exit, I nearly slam into a body and let out a yelp.

"Mag," I hiss, putting a hand over my heart and breathing deeply, "You scared the shit out of me."

The gargoyle grins at me, and I scowl. Mag is strikingly handsome with his tousled sandy-blond hair and light stubble. He wears a fitted black tee that accentuates his clearly defined muscles. All in all, an attractive package. Problem is he knows it.

At my scowl, his grin only widens, which proves my case.

"My presence is known to raise heart rates, Paige, I thought you'd be used to it by now," he says.

I roll my eyes and try to go around him, but he steps into my path.

"What do you want?" I ask, eyeing him warily.

Mag is a flirt. Something I sometimes find myself dishing right back if I'm bored, but the truth is that he is too much of a player for me. Though, I wonder if it's my refusal to fall for his charms that makes him try so hard.

"I was wondering if you've seen Blossom."

I snort. If Mag thinks I play hard to get, he certainly has his work cut out for him with the gorgeous unicorn shifter.

"Why? Didn't she offer to crush your balls into gravel the last time she saw you?"

He shrugs, his smile playful. "I like a challenge. And besides, I need to ask her for a favor."

"What favor would I possibly agree to do for you?" Blossom's biting tone cuts off my own reply—which would have been pretty much the same, for the record.

She steps into view from behind the stacks that lead to the poisonous creature section. There's a splatter of something bright blue on her elbow that makes me wonder if there was some sort of incident. Then again, I probably don't want to know.

Her gaze finds mine. "And it was sand," she says. "I offered to crush them into tiny sand granules."

I chuckle.

"Blossom, my beautiful friend," Mag drawls, completely unbothered.

Blossom glares. "I'm not your beautiful anything." She cuts me a look. "Is he bothering you? Because my job is to protect this library—and you—from all manner of threats. And from where I stand, the threat of assholery is *very* real."

"He was looking for you," I tell her.

"So... self-defense?" she asks sweetly.

I shake my head. "I can't approve it."

She sighs like I've really inconvenienced her by not letting her beat the shit out of him.

"Hilarious, you two," Mag says.

Blossom deadpans, "Who's joking?"

The strain between them is real, and I decide not to point out it feels awkwardly similar to sexual tension. Blossom would kick my ass if I uttered those words where

Mag is concerned. And Mag would never let her live it down.

The gargoyle has been a keeper of the Athenaeum for as long as I can remember. He's looked exactly the same as the day I met him, too. Basically, a poster child for the cover of GQ. And not a day older than twenty-five.

Humans would swoon, for sure. Honestly, supernaturals do too. One woman—a witch who'd lost access to her powers—actually *did* pass out while following him back to the moon magic section. She claimed low blood sugar, but the gnomes swear she was staring at his ass. Mag rode that high for months afterward.

Then, Blossom's arrival a year ago shook everything up, especially Mag, though he pretends to enjoy their rivalry. I don't think Blossom is pretending.

"Okay, look, I can see you aren't in the mood to grant favors," Mag says to her, "But I really need someone to cover my shift tonight."

"Hot date?" Blossom asks, her brow arching to let him know she finds that prospect doubtful.

"I'm flattered that you think so," he says.

"Everyone is lovable to someone," she says. "And I don't judge. I think you and Bingo make a cute couple."

I suppress a smile.

He clutches his heart, stagging back a step. "You wound me."

Her eyes glitter. "Not yet."

I shake my head, cutting in before blood can be

spilled. "Okay, before we make a mess on the newly cleaned rug, let's just agree Blossom is not going to cover for you."

"Someone gets me," Blossom says. "Now, if you'll excuse me, my shift is over, and there's a pint with my name on it waiting for me at my favorite tavern. Later."

She strides down the dimly lit hall before tossing her wrist out casually in front of her. The symbol tattooed on her skin glows to life, and a portal appears before her. She doesn't break stride as she marches right into the murky ether of the portal and then disappears.

Mag sighs and slowly turns away. "Great," he mutters.

"I'll do it," I blurt.

He stops and turns back. "Really?" Hope blooms in his light eyes then is quickly squashed as he shakes his head, gesturing to the tattoo on his wrist. "Keeper duties have to be done by someone with the mark."

"I won't tell if you won't."

"Look, if it were up to me, sure. I promised my little brother I'd show up for his playoff game tonight."

"You have a brother?"

"I have three."

"Oh."

I try not to seem surprised, but Mag never talks about himself, at least, not to me. He's the most mysterious person I've ever known, and considering the creatures that make up this place, that's saying something.

"Well, maybe you can ask one of the gnomes—offer them Sour Patch candy. That always works for me."

"Already did. It's Ned's birthday, so they're busy."

I bite my lip, all too aware of the opportunity this presents. "Look, the truth is I need this," I tell him. "I fucked up a few days ago, and Hoc's up my ass about it."

He smirks. "Is this about the troll? Because Blossom was pissed about her shoes."

"Ugh, don't remind me. Look, Hoc said it was my last strike, or I'm done here."

"Damn, kid. That's harsh."

I straighten. "If I can successfully hold down the fort on my own, Hoc will ease up, and maybe it'll win me some brownie points before graduation. Besides, I'm three weeks out. I'll be a full keeper soon enough, so it's not like I'm a total newb."

He hesitates, and I can see him considering it. I cross my fingers because this is seriously the best thing I know to prove to Hoc I can do this. The look of disappointment he gives me every time he sees me now is just too damn much to handle. Being a keeper might not be my dream, but I can't lose Hoc.

"I don't know," Mag says.

"Just take a couple of hours," I reply, talking far faster than normal. "It's not that long, but your brother will know you showed up. And besides, Bingo is here with me. I'm not completely alone. Worst case scenario, I'll release the hound." It's meant as a joke because we both know there is no way in hell—pun intended—I'm going anywhere near the obsidian dog with impenetrable skin and blazing red eyes.

Nope.

Definite pass.

Even with the keeper mark, that hound terrifies me.

Mag eyes me, considering.

"Two hours," he concedes, snapping me out of my thoughts.

I blink, eyes widening. "Seriously? Shit, thanks, Mag. You won't regret it."

His expression transforms, and suddenly, the easy-going playboy is gone, replaced with a stone-faced—and I mean that literally—gargoyle warrior. "I seriously hope not, Paige. Because if you get my ass busted, I will kick yours all the way through one of these dead-end portals, got it?"

I suppress a shudder. "Got it. You can count on me."

He looks unconvinced, especially considering he's just agreed to this. "I mean, seriously. I may adore you, but I *will* make you pay if you get me into trouble."

"I promise." I press a hand to my heart. "Scout's honor."

"You were never a scout," he replies. "That's a human thing."

"Heard it in a book once." I grin, and to my delight, Mag returns an annoyed smile. "One thing though," I say as he raises his wrist to conjure his own portal.

"What?"

My grin spreads. "I want a coffee. Strong, delicious, from somewhere other than my drip machine."

Mag groans. "You women never do anything out of the goodness of your hearts. Fine. Be back in a blink." Raising his wrist, he uses his tattoo to call the portal then disappears through it.

Envy is a taste on my tongue as I watch him go. My cozy apartment upstairs isn't bad, but the idea of being able to leave this place every night—to experience other worlds—is the only thing driving me to become a keeper.

That and instant access to the best lattes the worlds have to offer. Seriously, that could very much be the best job perk of them all.

Just over an hour later, my pace is slow and slightly wandering as I patrol the stacks with earbuds blaring. In one hand, I cup the pumpkin spice latte I negotiated from Mag. The other hand is free, prepared to deal with any mishaps *should* they happen.

They won't, though. It's been my silent mantra. The power of positive thinking and all that. Tonight is going to go down without a hitch, and tomorrow, I will be able to prove to Hoc that I do belong here.

That I can be the keeper he wants me to be.

As I walk, I sip. *Mmm.* Still warm. And so freaking

good. So far, the evening is proving quiet, and I'm already feeling the victory of a successful keeper shift under my belt—albeit a short one. Hopefully, Hoc will chill out and I'll be back on track to graduate from my internship. Hell, maybe they'll elevate me straight past novice if I play my cards right.

After the first hour passes with no books attacking me, I decide it's safe to pass the remaining time listening to an audiobook. The story of a slow-burn romance between a mafia crime boss and his female love interest, who is secretly his enemy's daughter, plays in one of my ears while I keep one earbud free. It's a forbidden love sort of thing. Human romance. But, damn, the heat level is off the charts.

"Please—" I beg.

"Please, what, Dee?" He stares down at me through hooded eyes while my own gaze travels down over his ripped abdomen and the massive bulge in his jeans.

"Please. I swear, I'm not spying on you."

"You see why it's difficult for me to believe you," Michael growls as he takes the tip of his finger and runs it along my cheek.

"What do I have to do to show you that I'm innocent? That my interest in you is purely my own?" I keep my chin strong, my tone level, because I want this man to see me as more than the daughter of his enemy.

I want him to see me as a woman.

He growls. "I can't say I dislike the sight of you on your knees. Pouty mouth ready for me." Michael's hand goes to my chin, and he runs the pad of his thumb over my bottom lip. "Will you show me that you're not wearing a wire?" He sticks the tip of his blade into the top of my shirt.

He cuts the fabric, and I suck in a breath as my shirt opens just enough to bare the swell of my breasts—and to show I'm not wearing anything but this low-cut lace bra. "Much better."

"Do you believe me now? Do you believe that I'm here because I can't stop thinking of you?"

He likes the power, and I have no problem giving it to him.

"That depends," he says softly.

"On what? I'll do anything."

He grins. "Then answer this." He sets the blade aside. "Are you ready for me, Dee? Ready for what I can give you?"

"Yes," I reply, breathless. "I've been ready since the moment we met."

He grins down at me and then undoes the button of his jeans. I'll do anything for him. On my knees, my back—whatever he desires, so long as he gives me the one thing I've never been able to find.

Connection.

I'm so wrapped up in the story, I almost miss the book that rattles to my left. When the movement catches my eye, I stop, turn, and swallow hard as it continues to move, jostling the books beside it.

"Oh no, you don't," I mutter as I glare at the leather-bound volume boasting the title *Sea Monster*. Which, let's be fair, is reason enough to hurry and shut the thing up.

With my non-coffee hand, I reach out and press my finger against the book's spine, whispering the word that will seal it shut. "Clauseruntque."

The book goes still just as the story I'm listening to picks up. Shit, I'm practically salivating at this point.

"I want to see that glorious body of yours," Michael demands.

"Anything for you."

With the misbehaving book back in its place, I take another sip of pumpkin spice—it's important to reward oneself for a job well done—and keep walking. While I keep a careful eye trained on the shelves, I listen with rapt attention to the scene playing out in my ear. The male continues questioning the heroine as he removes his pants. She swears—again—that she's not spying. He demands that she strip to prove she's not wearing a wire.

Uh-huh. Perfect sexy scene set-up.

I turn the corner to the next row of shelves, completely caught up as the man watches her remove her clothing. Sensually, of course.

When she's stripped down to nothing but her bra and panties, she stops. He growls for her to keep going. She refuses.

I turn down another aisle.

Mermaid section.

This area is usually pretty quiet. Maybe the characters inside know they'd be escaping to an atmosphere their gills can't handle. Whatever the reason, this section is usually my easiest.

Unconcerned, I quicken my pace, as the audiobook continues to build the heat.

"You have the body of a goddess," Michael tells me. And with the heat in his eyes, I believe him.

He reaches out and slips a finger beneath the lace panties I wear. Then, without asking for permission, he yanks and tears them from my body.

I gasp.

He slides a finger over me and moans. "So ready for me, Dee. So, damned ready."

The tension is ridiculous, and I decide right here and now to never settle for a guy who won't rip my panties off.

Ugh. Not that I know where to find one. And if I don't get access to those portals soon, I may never get the chance to look. Hoc's protectiveness is best described as Hoc-blocking.

I take another sip of my latte, sinking back into the story and living out my sex life vicariously through fictional characters.

A noise from up ahead snaps me out of it.

I hurry toward the creatures of the air section in time to see another book rattling.

The wyvern. Again.

This book likes to cause trouble, but tonight it seems especially full of itself.

The woman in my ear whimpers as the man yanks off her bra.

The book rattles harder.

Shit. Talk about a buzzkill.

With my free hand, I fumble for the pause button at the same moment the wyvern's book manages to tear itself loose and fly off the shelf. The cover shudders, threatening to open, and I forget about the story, racing for the book.

A screeching cry leaks out from between the pages, echoing in the ear that doesn't have a sexy scene playing out.

Wyverns are hideously high-pitched.

And this one is definitely going to get my ass busted if I don't hurry up.

The book shivers against the floor, jumping a few inches to the left. I almost miss it in its chaotic attempt to dodge me, but thankfully, I'm more agile than a three-thousand-year-old wyvern terror bound in leather.

Quickly setting aside my latte, I lunge as the book leaps and only barely manage to grab the thing out of the air. The wyvern screeches louder. I wince and proceed to wrestle the damn thing, stumbling left then right again. Through clenched teeth, I utter, "Clauseruntque."

With a final shove against my midsection, the book falls still.

Unfortunately, the momentum has left me in perpetual motion.

Careening backward, my shoulder hits the shelf behind me—hard.

I grunt, releasing the now-quiet wyvern book. It falls to the floor with a harmless thud—followed by several more muted thuds that have dread crawling up my spine faster than I can turn to see what's fallen.

"Shit," I hiss, bending low to grab the three other titles I've just knocked loose.

Maybe the books didn't notice. Maybe they won't even—

Before I can finish thinking the thought, the first book wakes.

The Mummy, it reads.

Dread coils in my belly. I've seen this movie. And there's no Brendan Fraser here to save me.

It trembles, and I panic. Throwing my entire body on top of the thing, I scream, "Clauseruntque!"

The book falls silent.

Something wet touches my ankle and I remember the latte. Twisting my body, I spot the offending pumpkin drink tipped over from the chaos and currently leaking onto the carpet.

With a heavy sigh, I reach for it, easing my weight off the trio of books I've yet to re-shelve. The moment I do, I realize my mistake.

A spine cracks open too fast for me to read the lettering. Pages blow by, and magic stirs the air. It snaps around me like an electric tornado, a whirl of color and sound that blocks out everything else.

"No!" I scream, no longer caring if someone hears because, in the next few seconds, I could be dead. "Hel—!"

My cry is cut short as a creature escapes straight from the pages of the story itself and into existence right in the center of the puddle of pumpkin spice.

CHAPTER 4
PAIGE

I brace myself, fully expecting a rukh or a harpy, or something equally vicious. That is my luck, after all. Instead, I see a man. My gaze travels over his angled face. *That jaw could cut glass.* His eyes, an impossible blue, shine brightly in the dim lights of the library.

Unashamed, I continue my perusal. He's standing still, so I drink him in, part of me waiting for him to strike, the other wondering if this isn't a figment of my imagination. Or maybe the audiobook has gotten into my head, made me finally snap from the sexual frustration.

Because, hot damn, this male is sex on a stick.

Brown hair falls to his broad shoulders in loose, damp waves that are just begging for me to run my fingers through them. Those shoulders lead to biceps that women can only *dream* about, which then connect to an expansive chest and rock-hard abs with more ripples than I can count.

Seriously, do this guy's abs have abs?

It's not until my eyes follow the perfect "V" of his hips and levels on a *massive* dick that I realize he's completely and totally naked. I'm struck stupid by the sight of it.

I mean. I've never seen one in person, so I don't have much to go off of, but I'm fairly certain this one would leave someone walking funny for *weeks*.

"Holy shit, you're naked." My face flushes because, screw manners, I cannot look away. Dude is hung like a horse. "You're not a horse-shifter, are you?"

He looses a short growl, which is the only thing that snaps me out of it. I lift my eyes back to his face, which seems an awfully long way up—what, with me still flat on my ass. The sight of his glare steals my breath—along with anything I might have said to further embarrass myself.

Then again, suffocating would probably be embarrassing too.

I should breathe. Maybe even say something.

But what?

Through the single earbud, the audiobook continues; the male lets his fingers glide over her clit, and she shudders, arching into his touch.

The male in front of me cocks his head, and I realize belatedly he must be able to hear what's coming out of the tiny pod in my ear.

Shit!

I yank on the pod, ripping it out. It falls onto the carpet, but that doesn't help. The sound continues to leak out, and I realize I still haven't paused it.

My phone!

Desperate, I yank my phone from my pocket and hit pause on the audio. The male reacts, flexing his arms and snarling viciously.

"Whoa, I'm just—"

I lean away, but apparently, he's decided I'm a threat because, in the next blink, dark scales appear along his arms and shoulders. When he exhales angrily, smoke curls from his nostrils, and I realize exactly what it is I've freed.

Dear gods. This is not happening.

I've just unleashed a fucking dragon. And he. Is. Pissed.

"Stop!" I screech. "If you shift, you're going to take the entire building down!"

To my complete surprise, the scales recede, and he remains in his human form. Though, given the massive dong between his legs and the amount of throbbing going on between mine, I'm not entirely sure that's the better option.

"Where am I?" he growls, his voice a deep baritone that does absolutely nothing to ease my attraction. I could *bathe* in that voice all damned day.

Pushing to my feet, I face him again, though given our

height difference, I barely make it to his expansive chest. A giant trying to climb into a clown car comes to mind, and I fight the urge to laugh. Maybe I *am* losing it.

"The Athenaeum," I manage.

"That's the name of this kingdom?"

"What? No, not a kingdom. It's—"

"What world am I in?" he demands.

"Earth," I say quickly. "You're on Earth."

"Humans?" His brows crinkle in confusion.

"You've been here?" I ask, surprised at the idea of a well-traveled naked dragon man.

"I've heard tales," he says darkly, which makes me think those tales weren't nice ones. "What magic brought me to this land?" he demands.

"Not land," I reply, retrieving my phone. "Library. And you came out of your book." *Oh shit.* It hits me again, lust dissipating. "Your book!" Turning, I grip it and hold it out to him, pages splayed open at random. "Go back inside. Now. You can't be here."

He eyes it warily. "That is a book."

"Yes. Clearly. Thank you for pointing it out. Now get back inside!" Aside from killing him, I'm not entirely sure how to get him back to his world. At least, not without a keeper tattoo and magic.

"I cannot go inside a book," the man replies, confusion marring his brow. The look in his eye suggests he's starting to question my sanity.

"Yes. You can. You came from it, which means you can

go back. Please. You have no idea how much trouble I'll be in if you stay."

"Trouble. Are you in distress?" He looks through the shelves to the other side as if seeking danger.

My alarm blares. *Oh fucknugget.* I'm out of time. The two hours Mag promised me are done—he'll be back any minute! And if he finds out, he'll *have* to report it. It won't matter that he left me here to cover his shift when I wasn't ready. He'll still tell Hoc, and then my three strikes are up, and I'm out on my ass.

Alone.

With no one.

And not even my memories to keep me company.

Interns who've had their minds wiped usually end up in mental institutions because they cannot remember who they are. Depending on how long they've been in the Anthenaeum, some are wracked with anxiety over what they *know* has to be out there.

Given that I've been here my entire life, chances are good that I'll suffer the same. Left alone, cold, and crazed in a world I can't even begin to understand.

"Fine. Never mind. We'll figure it out later. Come on." I grab his arm and try to drag him down the aisle, but he doesn't move. Instead, I'm jerked back against his hard body.

My blood heats.

Pulse races.

"You are clearly distressed," he says as he drops his nose to my neck and inhales.

"I will be if you don't come with me now." Pulling away, I face him. "Please. If Mag finds you, he's going to kill me."

"This Mag is trying to harm you?" His biceps bulge as he balls his hands into fists. Literally, bulge. Perfect. So, not only did I release a dragon, but I've also set free a stereotypical alphahole. The very same possessive, aggressive, muscle-bound hottie known as a book boyfriend.

"No. Not really." *Not if we haul ass.* "Will you please just come with me?"

He narrows his gaze then nods. "Very well."

Together, we half-run toward the stairs. By the time I make it to the second floor, I decide I deserve a freaking medal for not glancing over my shoulder even a single time to see that delicious body in motion.

Sexually tense Paige, zero—logical Paige, one.

Finally, I open the door to my apartment and shove the man inside then toss him his book. "Stay. Here."

"You said you are in danger," he says, already surging forward to follow me out again. "You should not go out alone."

I roll my eyes. "The only way I'm in danger is if you're with me. Stay here, and I'll be safe."

"I cannot in good conscience leave you to defend yourself against a threat."

"Fine, can you take an order from someone who's higher up on the food chain in this particular world?"

He frowns like he's never considered anyone being higher on the food chain. Which is fair. "Ugh. I will definitely get my ass kicked if anyone sees you right now. And that will ruin your chances of getting home. So, stay here, and I'll be right back. I swear it. Deal?"

He nods uncertainly, and I'm out the door again before he can ask the next question forming on his delicious lips. Like maybe how a girl without any shifter abilities to speak of could possibly be higher on the food chain than him.

I rush back down the stairs and grab a roll of paper towels from the library's kitchen before I bolt back toward my abandoned pumpkin spice. Mag is already standing in the aisle when I arrive. He stares down at the spill, his back to me.

Panic spears through me, but I shove it away and force myself to play it cool. "Hey," I call out.

He whirls, eyes narrowing at the sight of me. "Where the hell were you?"

"Sorry! Had to get something to clean it up."

He gestures to the books on the floor. Books that, thankfully, are still sealed. "Care to explain?"

"The wyvern acted up again, so I had to reseal the book. But I dropped my coffee and then went to get paper towels." I hold them up as proof even as the lie of omission tastes sour on my tongue.

Mag narrows his brow. "You got them all sealed?"

"Do you see any open?"

"I suppose not," he replies, though the suspicious gleam in his eye remains. "Thanks for covering."

"Sure. Of course. No problem." *I'm rambling.* "How did your brother do?"

"They lost," he replies. "But still a good game." Absently, he lifts the books and shelves them. "You're sure nothing else happened? The energy here, it's different."

"Likely from my stress," I joke. If the alarms didn't go off, it means the gnomes were far too busy to raise them. *Happy birthday, Ned.* So as long as I can get the dragon back into the book and Hoc was not in the library when it happened—which, if he were, he'd undoubtably be down here beside Mag—I should be fine.

Keyword being *should.*

"Sure. Well, thanks. I owe you one."

I kneel and sop up the spilled pumpkin spice. "Keep my spill a secret, and we'll call it even."

Mag grunts an agreement and then disappears into the stacks.

After throwing out the paper towels and now empty cup, I head back up to my apartment. Upstairs, I pause just outside the door and take a deep breath, heart pounding.

I will fix this.

All will be well.

Mood lifted by my confidence boost, I pull open the

door and am met with an eyeful of the best ass I have ever seen. In fact—same as with his massive peen—I've never actually seen a man's ass in person, but it's so damned perfect I feel educated enough to deem it the best ass.

World Class Ass. That's what it should be called.

He turns to face me, and I snap my gaze up to his face before I can get caught checking him out. Our eyes meet, and I still, his piercing blue eyes captivating me. "You are alive."

"Yes." I step inside and push the door closed then flip the lock.

His stare is more of a perusal like he's looking for something. It leaves me uneasy and strangely tingly in places I haven't ever tingled before.

"What?" I demand.

"You are unharmed," he adds, finally dragging his gaze back to mine.

I shiver. "Yeah." My mouth is suddenly parched, but I can't seem to make my feet move from this spot. "Are you okay?" I ask.

"This is a strange place," he says, eyeing the small living room and ignoring my question. "What is this?" He points to my fish tank.

"Bruno," I reply. "He's my fish."

"You cannot seriously get enough food from such a small creature."

I gape at him. "He's my pet! I'm not going to eat him!"

"A pet fish," he comments. "Interesting. You said I am in a library."

"Yes."

"Clearly, I am in another world. While I have heard fascinating stories of other places, I do not have time to explore. I need to return to my own. At once."

"I agree." Rushing over to his discarded book, I retrieve it from the couch and crack open the cover. Nothing happens. No stir of magic, no pulsating power.

Nothing.

The man watches me expectantly. "How do you return me?"

"I don't have the power to do that," I admit. "Only Hoc, Mag, or Blossom can—"

"Then let us go get this Mag," he snarls, rushing for the door.

"No!" I block him, throwing up both hands to stop him from going through me.

Instead, he runs smack into my hands. His flesh is warm beneath my touch, his heart racing against my palm. My mouth goes dry, the air around us shifting dangerously toward 'I want him to rip my panties off and fuck me dirty.' Which, of course, is asinine.

He is a supernatural creature from a book I'm supposed to protect the world from.

A dragon.

And I am an intern who will likely not even remember

this once Hoc discovers what I've done and wipes my memory.

"What is your name?" I ask, meeting his gaze and dropping my hands before I do something stupid and stroke him.

"Aries Nemos of Astronia," he replies. "Yours?"

"Paige Murphy, uh, of the Athenaeum."

"Paige Murphy," he repeats, my name magic on his tongue.

"Aries," I start. "I promise to get you home. I just need a little time to figure out how."

"Very well," he nods, stepping back. "I shall give you your time."

"Thanks." Breathing a sigh of relief, I clap my hands. "Now, let's get you dressed." I rush over to the small sewing table in the corner. Since I cannot actually leave the library until my internship ends and couldn't stand the thought of making Hoc shop for me anymore, I taught myself to sew.

Dresses, shirts, pants—I can make damn near anything.

Though, as I sit here and study his frame, my mind goes blank at the idea of covering up such a magnificent creature even though I know I have to. "Damn." My cheeks flush at the dirty thoughts I'm having. "Uh, I mean, I think I might need more fabric."

CHAPTER 5
PAIGE

Aries watches me while I work to put together a pair of pants large enough to accommodate his... size. I try not to notice the way his eyes track my movements like a predator watches prey, but even in stillness, he's formidable.

It's unnerving.

Maybe when he's dressed, it'll be easier. Because, as of now, my buffalo plaid throw blanket, while perfect for a night of couch sitting, is doing nothing to hide those damned delicious muscles. Hell, I'm surprised his dick fit behind it.

With precise movements, I position the fabric over the slide plate of my sewing machine. Over my shoulder, Aries looms closer, clearly being nosy about exactly what I'm doing here. I try to ignore him and focus on the project at hand. When I press the pedal at my foot to activate the needle, Aries jumps.

"What is that thing?" he demands.

I toss him a look, trying not to laugh at the startled expression he wears. "It's called a sewing machine."

"This ...sewing machine," he says, looking at the thing like it might jump up and bite him at any moment, "It makes clothing?"

"It made that jacket," I tell him, gesturing to the dark coat hanging on the peg beside my front door.

"I see." He frowns and goes back to merely staring over my shoulder while I work.

A moment later, I lift my foot off the pedal to reposition the fabric. In the silence, I can't help but ask, "You don't have machines where you come from?"

"Not like this. Ours do not make sounds like that. And we use needle and thread when we stitch clothing."

His answer makes me wonder just how many modern amenities they're going without in his world.

"And electricity? Do you have that?"

"What?"

"Light." I gesture overhead to the fixture currently illuminating my tiny living room.

He frowns. "We have gas-powered lamps but none that stick to the ceiling."

I can't help picturing a world stuck in medieval times with total Middle Earth vibes and perfectly toned warriors running around, willing and ready to defend a lady's honor. Clearly, reading human fiction is getting to me.

"What about running water?" I ask.

He stared at me. "Your water has legs? It can run like a man?"

I shake my head, a massively embarrassing snort escaping before I can stop it. Ducking my head, I turn back to the sewing machine.

"You must be very wealthy and important to have a fancy machine like this."

I shoot him a wry look. "Neither, actually. I'm pretty much the lowest-ranking person here. I'm an intern." At his blank look, I add, "A librarian."

"A librarian."

"That's right. And if I don't put you back into your book where you belong, I won't even be that." I pause, trying not to think too hard about what will happen to me if and when we're caught.

"You really think I came out of a story?" His tone is mocking, and I can't help but look up—straight into his enigmatic eyes. Buried in his dark gaze is wariness.

Right, like I'm the crazy one here.

I stand and stalk over to where his book is propped on the coffee table. Grabbing it, I march back to where he stands and hold it out.

"Here," I say. "Take it."

"For what purpose?"

"Read it. You can read, can't you?"

"Of course, I can read," he scoffs. "Everyone in Astronia is properly educated." The way he snaps the words makes it clear I've offended him.

"How wonderful for you all. Earth is still working on that."

He stares at me. For a second, I think he's going to ask about the Earth part, but instead, he takes the book and opens it to the first page. Scanning quickly, I watch as his doubt transforms into shock.

When he looks up again, he doesn't bother to hide his surprise. "This story is about Astronia. The war... the hoard. My father defeated them, drove them out of our lands." He flips pages, skimming sections in wonder. "It's all here. Even me." He looks awestruck. Dumbfounded.

It's kind of surreal; watching a character from a book read his own story. It's also expressly forbidden. But hey, we've come this far. When he looks up again, I can see that he believes me. Apparently, so much so that his next words make me instantly defensive. "You conjured me then."

"Whoa, there, Mr. Practical Magic, I did no such thing."

"But you are a witch?"

"No," I say, trying to hide my discomfort at this particular line of questioning. "Well, probably not."

His brow lifts, and I find myself explaining despite the fact that this kind of info isn't exactly something I share with just anyone. "I don't know what I am, really.

Twenty-five years ago, there was an incident here. They call it the Extrication. Long story. The point is, my book was destroyed but not before I was, well, extricated."

"You came from a story too?"

I nod.

"And your people?" he presses.

"Unfortunately, no one else from my world made it out, and so far, any supernatural abilities I may or may not possess have yet to make an appearance. Basically, we're not sure what I am."

"And you live here—in the library?"

"Above it, actually, but yes." I spread my arms wide to encompass my apartment. "Home sweet home."

"Alone?"

Something about the way he says it sends a tingle up my spine. Or, more accurately, up my thighs. *Damn sexy-ass storybook hero.*

"Yes," I say, forcing my voice even.

"You do not worry about danger or intruders?"

Honey, you can intrude me anytime.

"The magic protecting this place is pretty tight."

Tight, Paige, really?

"And if anything comes through" *—comes?? Ugh, Paige, stop it!—* "the keepers take care of it." I decide not to mention the gnomes. Or Bingo. My vow of secrecy has some boundaries. "Trust me, the Athenaeum can handle itself."

"You speak of this place as if it is a living, breathing thing."

"I guess it kind of is." I hesitate because this kind of info can get a girl fired and memory-wiped for sure, but Aries deserves to know where he's landed. "The Athenaeum is a library thought to be lost to the ages of time and destruction of war."

"I've never even heard of it."

"Secrecy is part of its protection. Some legends have called it the city of Atlantis. Other stories refer to it as the library of Alexandria. A few humans think they've cracked the code and now refer to it as the Akashic Records. Anyway, basically, every story containing every world and creature and event ever to occur in the multi-verse has a place here. The sections are endless."

"Sounds massive."

I can't help it, I glance at his junk barely covered by a buffalo plaid I'm not sure I'll ever wash again. *Okay. Now I'm grossing myself out.*

When I look back at his face, his brow is lifted high.

So busted.

I clear my throat and continue. "The area I work in is sort of what you'd call a prison, I guess. The books there hold a horror that, if unleashed, would threaten your world or mine, or both."

"And your job is to prevent that from happening."

I sigh, deciding to just go for it and explain the full history. I mean, why not? We've come this far.

"When the library was first created, a millennia ago, maybe more, the magic bestowed upon it was ancient and powerful. That magic is a life force of its own and keeps the library from becoming known, breached, or otherwise from falling. No witch can scry for it, no sorcerer can conjure it, and no portal will open to it except for those who wield the mark of the library itself."

"The library is its own well of power."

"Exactly."

He regards me carefully. "You truly did not conjure me then."

I sigh. "Truly."

I watch as his expression hardens into resolve. "In that case, we must find out what brought me here so we can learn how to return me to my world."

"Or we can skip directly to the part where I send you back."

"You say you don't know how."

"I don't, but somewhere in this library is the answer, and I'm just the girl to find it."

He doesn't look convinced. And while I can't blame him—right now, I'm just some random chick who is currently sewing him pants—I can't help but be a little put off by his lack of confidence. Does no one believe in me? Then again, why the hell am I surprised? I don't even believe in myself.

I finish off my current line of stitching and then hold up my masterpiece. The sweatpants material was supposed to be for a matching set for myself—top and bottom. But it's barely enough for one pair of bottoms for Aries. Still, stretchy waist, two leg holes that will hopefully cover his calves... they'll do.

"Put these on," I tell him, handing them over.

"What is it?" he asks, and I stop short at the horrified look he wears.

My brows lift. "Sweatpants."

His gaze flicks to me. "I've offended you."

"Look, I literally have nothing else to offer, and I am not sure my future self will agree, but I need you to cover yourself so I can look you in the eye." He hesitates. "They're popular in this world, okay?" I usher him into my bedroom before he can insult my creative ability further and shut the door.

While Aries navigates human clothes, I head for the kitchen. Not that I have any idea what a dragon eats, but hopefully, it's something frozen and laden with cheese because that's about all I've got.

With the oven preheating for a frozen pizza, I whirl toward the fridge and stop short. Aries stands in the kitchen doorway, the sweatpants riding low on his perfect hips. My blanket is in his hand, but I can barely tear my eyes from the delicious "V" leading straight down to an area I would love to get up close and personal with.

"Is this okay?" he asks.

Mother of...

"It's fine," I practically pant the word. "It's more than fine." *It's fucking delicious.*

I'm also aware I've just played right into the book boyfriend stereotype I snubbed my nose at earlier. Low-slung sweatpants below a perfectly shaped set of washboard abs? It doesn't get more basic than that. And I can't even be mad about it. Not now that I'm seeing it in the flesh.

"I can find something else," he says uncertainly. I've been staring too long. I know it; I just can't help it. He clears his throat. "Perhaps I should put this blanket back on—"

"No, no." I wave him off. "It's really fine. They look good."

So, so good.

I swallow hard.

"Are you preparing a meal?"

His question yanks me out of the thirst trap I'm caught in, and I glance at the pizza I've yet to put in the oven.

"Yes, preparing a meal," I say, trying to normalize my breathing as I go to work unwrapping the pizza. When that's done, I grab a bottle of wine off the counter. I look up in time to see Aries frowning at it.

"I prefer ale with mine."

"Oh, you prefer it, do you? I have White Claw and a bottle of Captain Morgan. Take your pick."

His expression is actually kind of hilarious. “You drink claws?”

“For the love of... here.” I grab the bottle of rum from the cabinet and hand it over.

He doesn’t move to take it, and I roll my eyes, going for a glass.

When he has both, he uncaps the bottle and pours a double shot. I watch as he tips it back and gulps it. Before I can catch myself, I’m struck stupid by the sight of his throat moving around the liquid, his Adam’s apple bobbing. The amount of muscle in his throat alone is—

“Not bad. This Captain Morgan knows his ale.”

I snort. “That he does.”

When he refills the glass and offers it to me, I shrug. “When in Rome.”

His eyes narrow. “This is sarcasm.”

I swallow down the burning treat and grin. “Ah, so they have that in your world.”

When the pizza is done, we eat on the couch. Two slices for me and the rest for the, apparently, starving dragon.

“That was adequate,” he says when the last crumb has been consumed. At my expression, he grins. “Sarcasm.”

I toss my napkin at him. He catches it, but his smile turns serious.

“This has been an enjoyable evening, Paige.”

My cheeks heat for no good reason. “Thanks.”

"But the fact is I have a kingdom that needs me. And I very much would appreciate your help in getting me back there."

Right.

"Look, I get it. This sucks for you."

"It is not ideal," he says carefully.

Not ideal. *Must* be a politician.

"But this isn't something I can figure out in one day."

"You said yourself the library will have the answers."

"Sure, but we can't just ask the question."

"I don't follow."

I sigh. "What happened tonight—it's dangerous. If anyone finds out..."

"You will get into trouble."

"Yes. But so will you."

He straightens, his chest puffing out. "I can handle myself."

I roll my eyes. "I'm not challenging your obviously superior strength, okay? But the people that work here are literally sworn to do whatever necessary to keep the stories contained."

"I'm not some story," he scoffs. "I'm a living being."

"You're a threat," I say, gentler now. "That's how they will treat you."

"I can take care of myself," he repeats. "But for your safety, I will not provoke them. Yet."

His words conjure images of another time, one I'm too

young to remember but are nonetheless stamped inside my brain, thanks to Hoc's stories.

"What is it?" he asks at my expression.

"Look, the only time anything like this has happened was the day I arrived."

"This extrication business," he supplies.

"Yes."

"And that was very bad?"

"Very."

"I don't understand. You said you came from a story, and yet here you are, accepted as one of them."

"I was an exception to the rule, believe me." I don't bother to point out that if I hadn't been a helpless baby, Hoc probably would have ordered me killed too.

"And what is the rule?"

"Everything that escaped its book was hunted down —and destroyed."

CHAPTER 6
ARIES

"Destroyed?" I nearly growl it, anger heating the blood within my veins. Has this petite woman slaughtered innocents who, like me, were ripped from their homes—their worlds—through no fault of their own?

The moment that thought crosses my mind, though, I dismiss it. The expression on her face is not one of malice or guilt. Rather, she looks distressed. This is not a woman who has ever taken a life, evidenced by the horror reflected in her soft brown eyes and the fact that she is hiding me in her tiny home.

"Yes," Paige replies.

And though her tone is grave as she answers me, I cannot help but notice my own body's reaction to her presence. A reaction I've been ignoring since the moment I landed in this strange world. Paige is beautiful with her honey-colored hair and piercing yet innocent eyes. But it's more than her beauty that stirs my blood—that stirs my dragon.

The very sound of her voice is music to my ears. She calls to me, beckoning to a part of me no female has reached—until now. The beast in my veins desires her. But his need to claim her makes no sense.

This woman is not from my world. Therefore, she cannot be *mine*.

"What types of creatures were they?" I question, hoping to keep my mind from the very clear mistake my dragon has made. Trapped here in this strange world, the last thing I need is to become distracted by lust.

"I don't know," she tells me as she pushes her glasses up her nose and begins to pace. "I was too young to remember, but based on what Mag has told me—"

"Mag." The anger returns. "The one you feared would harm you?"

She shakes her head, letting out an adorably frustrated sigh. "He won't hurt me. At least, not on purpose." Paige turns to face me, her arms crossed, which sends her delicious cleavage nearly spilling from the top of her shirt.

My cock hardens, and I take a seat on her plush couch since these damned pants do nothing to hide my clear arousal. Not that she notices; far too wrapped in her own worries, Paige stands and begins to pace.

Something I am quite grateful for since it gives me ample opportunity to study her flawless, round ass. Its shape is set on perfect display in the tight pants that are apparently custom for females in this land. *Damn this temptress. Was she lying? Is she a witch who has enchanted me?*

"I was too little to remember the Extrication, but Mag told me that there were dozens of creatures on the loose. Said it took them weeks to track them all through the library."

The picture she paints yanks me from my distraction, and I glare at her. "Innocent lives taken because they were ripped from their worlds? Were they even a threat? Or simply in the wrong place?" I snarl along with the words. My thoughts instantly shift to the people of my world. To the knowledge that they would be hunted and slaughtered all because they were unknowingly pulled from their homes.

She stares at me blankly. "I—I don't know. From what I've heard, they were all highly combative. A word Mag used," she adds.

"Not something I can blame them for," I retort. "In fact, I would almost enjoy seeing this Mag try to—how did you put it?—destroy me. I think I would be rather *combative* if someone were trying to slaughter me as well."

Paige pales slightly. Whether it's my challenge or the risk to this Mag that caused it, I don't know. But I cannot be bothered to find out. Not when I have a home to return to and a kingdom to run.

"He's not going to get the chance," she says. "Because

he's never going to know you're here." The woman crosses toward me and drops to her knees at my feet.

My blood stirs, lust shooting through me like a punch. How easy it would be to pull her into my lap. To claim those plump lips with my own. Or let her stay where she is, sliding my pants down while she lowered her mouth onto my—

"Please, just give me time. I need to find a way to get you home *safely*. The people here, they're only doing their jobs, but if they find you—"

"Their job is to kill me. You've made that quite clear."

Paige takes a deep breath. "Please, Aries."

Nearly shuddering at the sound of my name from her lips, I consider her request. While I do not believe anyone here possesses the power required to match me in strength or speed, this is a world I am unfamiliar with. I have no weapons, no allies. Therefore, challenging anyone could be a potentially deadly mistake.

Getting home to save my family outweighs my prideful desires. "Very well. I will allow you time to find a way to send me home. But I must return," I add, staring into her depthless gaze. "My family is counting on me. My *world* is counting on me."

Paige swallows hard. Her gaze flicks down to my mouth then back up to my eyes so quickly I nearly miss it. *Mine.* The single word runs through my mind, but I beat it down.

Coming here must have fucked up my senses because,

in my world, in my home, this woman is not my mate. She cannot be. And there is too much at stake should I choose wrong.

"Thank you." She stands and crosses to her kitchen to fill a glass of water from the tap.

I follow, transfixed by the clear water pouring from the silver tube. "What magic is this?" I reach around her to turn it on then flick it off again. The water stops and starts with the move of a lever. It's magic, though I've never seen an enchantment quite like this before.

"Umm, running water?" Her close reply catches me off guard, so I look down, surprised to see she's standing between me and the sink, a mere breath away. Her eyes lock on mine, her warm gaze traveling over my face just as mine does hers.

This woman is beautiful chaos. I've known her for less than an evening, and already I know that she is the exact opposite of the mate my mother has described me needing.

But when I see her—

My thoughts die in that moment because Paige grips my neck and yanks my mouth down to hers. Her lips are soft and pillowy. Inviting, even as all logic dictates I pull away. An inner warning that disappears as her tongue runs along my lips, beckoning them to open. My beast stirs as I sweep my tongue over hers and forget all the reasons why this is unthinkable.

In fact, I stop thinking at all.

Reaching down, I grip that perfectly round ass and set her on the counter. Moving between her legs, I keep my mouth firm on hers, my hands sliding up her sides and skimming those perfect breasts I long to hold in my hands.

Her nipples are hard as I graze them through her shirt, and she leans further into me. I slide my palms up her neck, cupping the sides of her face, and bury my fingers in the thick strands of her sunlit hair.

Paige is an explosion of flavor. Heady cinnamon with a punch of Captain Morgan's ale. My cock is so hard it's damn near painful. And when the delicate scent of her arousal slams into me, I nearly lose the battle to resist my urges.

Mine.

Paige moans, soft and throaty. I press up against her hot core, my promise of what's to come.

At my intimate touch, she stills. Her mouth leaves mine, and she squeezes her eyes shut as if the separation pains her. With both hands, she presses against my chest and shoves me back. I stare at her, our breathing ragged.

Her eyes open, her gaze colliding with mine. Immediately, her cheeks redden, and she covers her face. "Whoa! Holy shit, I am so sorry," she wails.

"Sorry?" I echo, thoroughly confused.

She jumps down from the counter and shakes her head. "Stupid, stupid, stupid," she mutters to herself. "Gotta stop listening to those audiobooks." Muscles quivering, she continues to shake. Fear pushes through my lust.

What if she is ill? Where is the nearest healer in this world? How will I help her? "Are you all right?" I question, reaching for her. "Do you need to see a healer? Is something wrong?"

"Wrong?" She looks back at me, dazed, lips swollen from our kisses. "Ugh." She shakes her head and mutters, "My nipples are so hard they might shred this shirt, but—oh fuck, I did *not* just say that!" She shakes her head, her gaze darting everywhere but mine.

I study her, trying to understand the reason for her misery. Lips puffy and red from our kiss, she looks utterly delectable. Already I yearn for another taste.

"Listen. That was a mistake. I'm sorry. It won't happen again."

I don't reply, both dumbfounded by the fact that it was she who stole the kiss in the first place and the fact that the bond I feel for her just grew tenfold after touching her just once.

Now it's my turn to feel the cool claws of fear. *What if—*

"Use the blanket from earlier. You can sleep on the couch," she says, interrupting me. Paige starts to go and then turns back, adding, "Please don't leave while I'm asleep." Then she spins on her heel and marches across the room to the bed chamber where she'd had me dress.

She slams the door behind her while I remain standing, staring after her like a fool.

In the long moments that follow, I realize she's not coming back. Not tonight. And the realization leaves me strangely lonely. I've kissed women before. Shared the beds of willing females even as we both knew it was going nowhere. But this? This is the first time a woman kissed *me*.

The first time I've felt with absolute certainty that a woman was meant to be mine. Even though, realistically, I know she cannot be.

It makes no sense. Why would my beast choose someone who can never be mine? Why put us both through the misery of a bond when nothing can come from it?

I cross over and sit on the couch, staring at the shadowy wall across from me.

Paige and I are worlds apart, and I'm not sure even my dragon can remedy that.

CHAPTER 7
PAIGE

I sleep like shit, tossing and turning until I nearly give in and grab my earbuds with the idea that listening to an audiobook might help. But then I remember what a disaster that led to last night. And nearly the day before that, if I'm being honest.

Ugh.

Hoc was already right once—saying that my audiobooks were a dangerous distraction. I'm not going to make that true a second time.

I groan, the throbbing between my legs growing tenfold when I picture the tall, hot, and half-naked dragon currently sleeping just outside my room. I swear, I think my blue balls are worse than any male's. Years' worth of listening to other people get theirs has left a giant dick-sized hole in my heart—or something like that.

Finally, the light outside my window begins to change

with the coming dawn. It lures me like a Bat-Signal, and I toss back the covers to stumble over to the view. My sheer curtains are a formality; I know full well the glamour that protects this building is impenetrable. To the outside world and the humans in it, the walls housing the Athenaeum appear droll and forgetful. Sure, the architecture matches the rest of downtown Boston, a description that lands somewhere between classical Colonial and modern rehab. But the magic is about more than appearance. It's about the literal repulsion it causes anyone who looks directly at it. The moment they try, something in their mind directs them away again.

The human mind is such a fragile thing, easily influenced and awfully short-sighted. The real irony is that most don't even need the magic to pass us by without a second thought. Their obsession over their own lives—the self-centered immersion they feel toward their devices and their own petty problems—is protection enough.

I wouldn't have believed it if I hadn't born witness to it my entire life from this very window. I've spent hours studying human behavior from this very spot, and my conclusion is that, while living up here can be lonely at times, I don't belong down there. I'm not one of them.

That doesn't mean I don't appreciate the scenery their world has to offer.

The view, beyond the pedestrians crossing this way and that, is stellar. Today, the hazy morning offers no more than a glimpse of the harbor that lies at the end of this busy street. I've never been out there, but Hoc assures me it's not worth the trip.

Something I seriously doubt.

Worth it or not, I'm stuck here. As much a part of the Athenaeum as any book on its shelf. A prisoner in this opulent jail cell.

Turning away from the window, I shower and dress. My house guest hasn't made a sound from the living room, and I alternate between wanting him gone forever and worried he left after my stunt last night.

But *damn.* That kiss. *That* was the lip-smacking, world-tilting, heart-racing, panty-dropping thing of romance novels. Unfortunately, I'm all too aware that mine is not a love story.

By the time I emerge from my bedroom, I feel slightly more in control. A leather jacket and charcoal eyeliner tend to do that—or at least offer me an illusion of it, anyway.

Aries is sprawled on the couch, and I breathe a sigh of relief that he's still here. Though, maybe I shouldn't be happy about it. I still have to get through today without anyone finding out what I've done. Maybe admitting my mistake to Hoc is the best way to handle this. Maybe he can—

No. I shake off the thought immediately, fear clogging my throat. Hoc has never shown an inch of mercy where the books are concerned. And I can't stomach the thought of Aries getting hurt.

I tell myself it's because it's my fault he was ripped from his world. That if he is hurt or killed for my transgression, then his death will weigh fully on my shoulders.

But I know that if I examine that reasoning closer, I'll see that it's something else entirely. So, I do what I do best: I ignore it and make my way to the kitchen to start the coffeepot. After all, caffeine fixes everything.

Like *Windex* in *My Big Fat Greek Wedding.*

The rustling of a blanket on the couch sends a jolt through me. I don't look up, though. Not even when I hear him come into the kitchen. My skin prickles with the sensation of his gaze on me, but I concentrate on pouring the coffee, mixing the cream.

Aries doesn't say a word. Somehow, that's worse.

Finally, there's nothing left for me to do but turn and face him. With a mug in each hand, I do just that, with the addition of plastering a stiff smile on my face.

"Morning," I say, way too chipper for a girl who threw herself at a man-god last night with absolutely zero shame.

"Good morning," he says, studying me warily. I can't blame him. He likely can't decide whether I'm going to jump him or not. Shit, what if he has a girlfriend back home? A wife?

Mortification sneaks up my spine. "Coffee?" I hold out a mug; a peace offering.

He takes it and sips gingerly at first. His eyes widen. "This is good."

I smirk. "I'm not much of a cook, but I can make a hell of a cup of java."

"Java," he repeats as if committing the word to memory. How the hell can this man make that word sound so sinfully sexy?

I sip my coffee, letting the caffeine do its thing to hopefully clear my head. "So, listen. I'm sorry about last night. I can't imagine your girlfriend would have appreciated me attacking you like I did."

His brows furrow, and I hate that it's so damned adorable. "Girlfriend?"

"Wife, then?"

"I am not married," he replies. "I haven't found my mate yet."

Mate. Of course! Dragons mate for life. Like wolves, vampires, and nearly every other supernatural. Everyone but me, apparently. "Oh. Well. Then, I'm sorry. For attacking you."

Aries's eyes blaze like blue fire. "I did not feel attacked."

Damn. "Good. Still. Sorry."

"Understood." He takes a drink of his coffee. "How are you feeling this morning?"

"Great." *Lie.* "You?"

He frowns, and something flickers behind his dark gaze. "This world is loud."

"Is it?" I cock my head, listening to the muted sounds of traffic from the street outside. "I don't notice it."

I gulp more coffee, checking the time. Considering the level of awkwardness in this kitchen, maybe today will be my first time arriving early to work. I set aside my mug, deciding to get more when I'm downstairs, and head for the door.

Aries does the same. "Where are we going?"

"Whoa, not we," I say, stopping short and holding up my hand. "Me." I pull my hand back before his bare chest can run into it. I'm strong but not that strong.

"I cannot stay here," he says, and if I weren't so determined to get away from his sexy ass, I might smile at the way he's pouting.

"That's exactly what you're going to do." He opens his mouth, clearly determined to argue, so I press on. "Remember our talk last night? No one can know you're here."

"Or they will hunt me. Yes, yes, I remember." But he doesn't look even close to agreeing with me on this.

I sigh. "I know it's not ideal and my place is kind of small, but you have to stay here today."

"And where will you go?"

"Downstairs. I have to work. If I don't show up for my shift, Hoc will come looking for me."

His eyes narrow. "Who is this Hoc?"

"He's like my dad," I say, struggling to explain

without triggering a million more questions. "And he runs the library."

"I thought the library runs itself."

"It does. But he's the head librarian in charge of making sure everything remains in order." And the books remain shut. Ugh.

"So he is your superior?"

"Yes."

"And your father?"

"I need to go down and pretend everything's fine," I say, dodging his question.

"And then you will return," he says uncertainly.

"As soon as my shift ends, I'll be back. And tonight, once Hoc leaves, we can work on finding a way to get you home."

He grunts, clearly not a fan of staying put. I walk over and pick up the remote, powering on the television. The screen comes to life—a baseball game. Aries' eyes widen as he stares at the screen. Human amenities for the win.

"What is this miracle?" he breathes.

"Baseball."

"Baseball?" He takes a step toward the screen.

"A re-run of last night's game. If you want something different, hit this button," I tell him, shoving the remote into his hands. "I'll check on you soon."

He doesn't respond, and I decide now is as good a time as any to make my exit. Here's hoping dragons like daytime TV.

I'M SO LOST in my own thoughts that Blossom nearly gives me a heart attack when she corners me in the vampire section and says, "I know what you did last night."

My legs threaten to buckle right there as I squeak, "What?"

She glares at me. "You covered for Mag," she hisses.

"Oh." I exhale, thoroughly relieved, which only makes her seem to glare harder.

"Oh? That's all you have to say? Paige, you know you aren't cleared for keeper duty."

"I know. I just thought maybe..." I trail off, fully aware of how stupid it will sound now that I'm saying it aloud. Especially given what actually happened last night.

The scope of my fuck up knows no bounds. Which means I am not the keeper I thought I could be. And that realization hits. Hard.

"You thought Hoc would forgive your little stunt last week if you played grown-up?" Her words are snarky, but her tone lacks all condescension. She's worried about me. And that makes me feel even worse.

"Maybe."

She smirks. "I mean, it's not the worst idea." Her smile drops. "Unless, of course, a book decided to make a break for it."

Oh shit. I try not to wince. "Nothing happened."

"Hmm." Her reproachful look lasts another few

seconds, and then, like a switch being flipped, she lets it go and moves on. "What was Mag doing, anyway? Was it buy one get one free hooker night or something?"

I snort as we fall into step together, patrolling the stacks. "No idea. You know how mysterious he is."

"Shady, you mean."

I don't tell her about his brother's playoff game. I've known Mag my whole life, and last night was the first personal detail he's ever shared with me. As trivial as the detail may be, I can't bring myself to break his trust when he's only so recently given it to me.

Blossom doesn't seem to notice, though. For the next half hour, we chat about her. More accurately, she chats, and I listen. Blossom is here as punishment for breaching a portal from her world to another—a grave offense by any world's standards, but entry into this one was apparently extra forbidden. She snuck through a portal that led to a world full of unicorn shifters like her. Or so she'd thought. Except that, when she'd arrived, all she'd found were remains.

The world had died off hundreds of years ago, and no one had told her.

I suspect her rage at being sentenced here as a keeper is partly a cover for her sorrow. I can't blame her. All she'd wanted was to know where she came from, to find her own kind. Instead, she'd learned how truly alone she is. And now she's stuck here, tasked with making sure no one else leaves their world either.

It sucks.

So, I let her complain until we break for lunch. At least, it takes my mind off the dragon currently discovering the American pastime of baseball in my apartment.

I'm so lost in my own thoughts that I don't notice Hoc until he's come into the break room behind me and blocked the exit.

"There you are," he says, and I jump, the move sending lettuce and tomato flying as I nearly drop my salad.

"You startled me," I say, gasping for breath. Heart pounding, I hurry to clean up my mess.

"Are you all right?" Hoc asks.

"Fine," I say, "Great. What's up?"

"I haven't seen you all morning."

"Busy day," I say, way too chipper.

"Right." He hesitates.

I force myself to meet his eyes, focusing on my breaths. Hoc is supernatural with senses to match. If he notices my heart rate is trying out a techno beat, he'll know something's up. "Is there something else?"

"I only wanted to say I'm very proud of you for the work you're doing." He softens. "The smooth past couple of days are a testament to your commitment and ability. Keep this up and you'll be elevated to keeper, I'm sure of it."

The guilt nearly drags me to my knees. "Thank you," I tell him.

“I saw the report this morning,” he goes on. “Mag had a near-miss last night.”

“Oh?” My voice comes out way too high.

“When I asked him about it, he admitted the long shifts are getting to him. We are definitely spread thin here. I think we’re all looking forward to adding you to our ranks to help balance things out.”

“I’m just glad everything is in order,” I tell him. The lie is bitter on my tongue. Letting Mag take the fall for my fuck up—even if no one here knows the full gravity of it—Mag included—is so damn wrong.

But Mag isn’t on his last strike.

And Mag won’t have his memory wiped if he fucks up one more time.

I am, and I will. So, I let it slide and make a mental note to owe him a shit-ton of covered shifts once I do finally become a keeper.

“As am I. The last thing we need is another extrication on our hands. I’m too old to slay anything anymore.” He pauses, and I shudder, thinking of Hoc and Aries coming to blows. “Anyway, keep up the good work.”

I offer a slight nod. “Will do,” I call as he walks out.

When he’s gone, I sink into the plastic chair and stare down at my salad as if it’s my last supper. One wrong move and it damn well will be. I have to get Aries home—tonight. Both our lives depend on it.

CHAPTER 8
ARIES

On the tiny box in Paige's living room, men hit the ball with a strange blunt stick. The crowd goes wild, jumping to their feet and screaming like madmen as the ball soars through the sky. They cheer even louder when the man who hit it drops his stick to run in a wide circle.

Truthfully, it makes no sense. But it is quite intriguing to watch what passes for entertainment in this world. Back home, if there is not a blade being used, it is rarely considered crowd worthy.

My stomach rumbles. Shit. Did she tell me what to do should I get hungry? So far, I haven't seen a single servant. Pushing to my feet, I make my way into her kitchen, toward the white box that made a mind-numbing humming sound all night.

After gripping the handle and pulling it open, I'm

blasted with a gust of cold air that has the hair on my arms standing on end. Like winter when the rest of the apartment feels like autumn. *Interesting.* I lean in closer, feeling the icy air on my face and smiling.

What other fascinations might this world hold?

Reaching into the winter box, I withdraw a yellow block. It's firm, though when I open the bag containing it, it appears to be soft enough to be sliced through. Turning in a slow circle, I look for a blade. With a victorious smile, I spot a wooden block boasting some knives.

After setting the yellow block on the counter, I slice a chunk off and take a bite. The taste is familiar even if the color seems—well—off.

"Strange-looking cheese," I comment as I continue munching then return the cheese to its bag and place it back in the fridge.

A few minutes later, I'm trekking toward the couch with my bounty—more cheese, some small, square, chunks of salty, dried bread, and an ale. The baseball game is now over, and in its place is a bunch of men sitting around a table, talking about things called 'stats'.

Curious what other forms of entertainment might be inside this small box, I hit the button Paige showed me earlier. The screen goes black less than a second before another picture appears.

A man claims a woman's mouth, his hands on her shoulders. It brings to mind a similar moment from last night when Paige kissed me. My body warms at the thought, and I recall the memories of my dreams spent buried inside her.

Never has a woman had such an effect on me. If I were home in Astronia, I might even be tempted to consider my feelings for Paige to be the mating call. But that's impossible. We're from different worlds, her and I. And that's how it must remain. Even if I had to fight the urge to slip into her room and see just how far that kiss could have taken us.

I'm ripped from my thoughts when the man onscreen pulls away from the woman.

"Did my brother kiss like that?" he demands. Brother? What the hell? A woman should not be kissing brothers!

"How dare you speak to me like that," the woman screeches before her hand cracks across the man's cheek.

He rushes forward and grips her arms then slams her into the wall.

Anger burns in my throat even as I am helpless to tear my gaze from the scene. How the hell do I get inside and save her? How do I—

"How dare I speak to you like that? How about the fact that you went to that ski lodge in Aspen with my brother?" he bellows.

I abandon my food on the small table then lean in closer as though somehow that might aid me in hearing clearer. Surely this woman was not traipsing off to unknown lands with this man's brother if she's supposed to be with him!

"I thought he was you!"

"How can you say that! After everything we've been through, how could you not know it wasn't me? I am your husband!"

"You are identical twins, Micah. And he—" She closes her eyes, and a tear rolls down her cheek. *"He romanced me! Bought me flowers the same way you used to! And when we were together—"*

The man jumps back as though she struck him again. *"You slept with him?"*

The woman sniffles. *"Yes. And he was a far better lover than you!"*

"And now he's dead," the man says. *"You killed him!"*

She lets out a horrified scream then turns away and begins to sob. *"He never saw that tree, Micah. He never saw it."*

"Damn," I murmur, already far more engulfed in this drama than I was in the baseball. Grabbing my food, I lean back and prepare to see just how this woman manages to talk herself out of the offense of sleeping with her mate's brother.

"WHAT THE HELL ARE YOU WATCHING?"

I turn my head to study Paige as she stands above me, arms crossed. Her hair is braided over her shoulder, her glasses perched atop a perfectly straight nose. Both dark eyes are narrowed on me.

"That woman slept with her mate's twin brother, and then the offending man died. Then a different man impregnated his mate's mother. It's quite an interesting stream of events. One wouldn't think so many lives could have these many transgressions in them."

The corners of her lips twitch, and she reaches down and presses a button on the remote. The wording *Minutes of our Days* pops up along the top of the screen. "You're watching a soap opera?"

"Soap opera?" The words are unfamiliar strung together that way. "Is that what this is? Either way, these people would not survive a day in my world. Most of them would have been put to death due to fear that their insanity is contagious."

She snorts, selecting a button that mutes all sound on the screen, and sets the remote down. "It's fiction, Aries."

"Fiction?"

"Fake. Not real."

"I know what fiction is, Paige. We do have books in my world." My brow furrows as I stare at the magic box. "So these are simply fake stories being acted out?"

"Theatre, my friend," she replies then plops down on the couch beside me and runs both hands over her face.

"Ahh, that makes much more sense."

Paige yawns and drops her hands, but her eyes remain closed. It gives me the perfect moment to study her profile. She's gorgeous, stunningly beautiful in the way she carries herself.

There's something about her that calls to me. That calls to the dragon in my heart. My gaze drops to her mouth. Those perfect, plump lips I'd had on mine just last night. My cock stiffens in my pants as lust pummels me.

Clearing my throat, I avert my gaze back to the muted box. "How was your day?"

"Fine. Long. Stressful." She groans. "We're going to have to be super careful tonight. Blossom is on duty, and her senses are never far off." Paige rolls her shoulders, and my fingers flex.

"May I?"

She cracks open an eye and stares at me. "May you what?"

"I can rub the tension from your shoulders. You can hardly be expected to remain focused on the task at hand when you're tense."

Her gaze narrows. "Are you trying to get handsy with me, Aries? Because, I have to warn you, I have no intention of continuing last night's mistake. I already apologized. And I make it a habit of not being a repeat offender."

I offer her a smile even as disappointment battles with logic. "Neither do I," I say. "I am merely offering to help you so we can be fully focused on getting me home."

She continues to watch me, mouth flattened in a tight

line, until finally she nods. "Fine. But your hands stay on my shoulders, got it?"

"Of course," I say, dipping my head in a nod. I spread my legs apart as Paige stands and kneels before me.

Heart pounding, I reach up and brush the strands of her thick hair off of her shoulders then take a deep breath and begin to knead. Her muscles are tense beneath my fingers, and as I work to remove the knots, it takes nearly all of my strength to keep my word. Especially when she lets out a low moan and her head tips forward in obvious pleasure.

"That feels amazing," she groans.

"You are quite tense."

"Yeah, well, I released a dragon into the world last night. Sue me."

"Sue you?"

"Figure of speech." She groans. "Seriously, though, your fingers are magic."

I start to respond. To tell her that my fingers cannot be magic, but then her scent changes. The arousal coming off of her hits me like a stone to the head, and my hands tighten their grip on her body. Everything about her begs to be possessed.

To be touched.

Tasted.

Thanks to my senses, I can damn near taste her on my tongue all over again. And it's not nearly enough. My beast surges beneath my skin, his desperation for her growing as well.

"Aries?"

"What?"

"You're holding me pretty tight," she says with a half laugh.

Releasing her and standing before I do something stupid, I put some distance between us. "Should you clean up before we go?"

Paige stands and narrows her gaze on me. "Do I stink?"

More like you smell so damn good I want to devour you until you're screaming my name as you come. "No, I am simply unsure what your typical routine looks like."

"Typically, I'm not sneaking through the library, avoiding my crazy, astute friend while I try to find a way to get a dragon I inadvertently released back home."

My mouth quirks into a slow smile. "Understood."

She glances back at her bedroom then turns to me. "I'll go change into something more comfortable, though. Are you hungry?"

"I ate." My response is far sharper than I meant it to be, but it cannot be helped. She is making me question the very fate I know will save my people. I am to be with my mate. The one person who was made exclusively for me, and I, her. Given that she is not from my world, I know it cannot be her.

Yet, wanting her this way—

"Okay. Well, I'll be out soon." She offers me a smile then turns and disappears into her room. I let out a breath and run a hand through my hair. I must get home tonight.

Otherwise, I fear that my attachment to this woman might make leaving near impossible.

CHAPTER 9
PAIGE

By the time I re-emerge from my bedroom, wearing my favorite leggings and an oversized sweatshirt, no less—I'm pretty convinced Aries is a hypnotist. What other explanation is there for how he's gotten so far inside my head?

I've known him less than twenty-four hours, and already, all I think about is him. His broad shoulders and muscled biceps. The way his hair curls over his forehead. The bright, hungry eyes that seem to see through to parts of me I don't even recognize myself.

It's a little terrifying how much he's consumed me—and that's saying a lot, coming from a girl who's battled a literal poltergeist.

Then I reach the living room and realize, no, hypnotist is the wrong word. Aries is a damned thirst trap. He's wearing the sweatpants I made for him, slung low, and no shirt to cover his rippled abs. On top of that, he's found an old ball cap Hoc gave me once—except he's turned it backward. The air leaves my lungs—and my ovaries.

"What is that?" I ask in a strangled voice.

"This is what they wore in The Baseball."

"Right, look, I can't... ugh." I double back to my bedroom and grab an oversized tee from the bottom of my dresser. Then I march back out into the living room and toss it at the eye candy. "Put that on so I can look at you."

I wait while he removes the hat and pulls the shirt over his head. When the shirt is in place—albeit tight, but at least, he's covered—I exhale.

"Do you like it?" he asks, adjusting the hat that's now firmly back in place.

"Do I...?" I try to swallow but it gets stuck. "Yeah," I manage. "It works."

"Good. You look nice too," he says. "In our world, women don't wear pants in public, but I must admit the look suits you." His gaze darts to my waist, and my cheeks heat.

"Thanks." I do my best to get my bearings. Focusing on the wall instead of his dreamy face, my scattered thoughts slowly reform. "We should get going. We need to find a book that will explain the process to us and—shit!" My eyes land on a familiar item across the room.

"What is it?"

I groan. "We need to put your book back. I can't believe I forgot about it."

"My book?"

I grab it off the coffee table and tuck it under my arm. "Yes. Hoc mentioned he saw a report of a near-miss last night, and that means he'll probably ask Blossom to patrol your area with extra care tonight. If she notices a book missing, it won't take long for them to figure out what happened."

"But don't we need my book in order to send me home?"

"We'll have to double back for it once we've found the spell to make it all work."

"And where will that be found?"

"If I knew, we wouldn't have to look, would we?"

He frowns. "Sarcasm again?"

I sigh. "Come on."

"Wait."

His sudden urgency stops me.

"What is it?" I ask, facing him again.

He looks at me expectantly. As though I should already know just what it is he's going to say. "I'll require a weapon."

"A what?"

"Should we encounter a threat, I'll need to neutralize it. And for this, I'll need a weapon. I came through without any of my own—"

"Whoa there, killer. No weapons tonight. Our mission

is to complete the objective without any encounters. Do you understand?"

"I need to be able to protect you," he says, and for some reason, I'm touched. It's ridiculous because no way can I condone violence, but some part of me—lady parts, mostly—find his intention endearing.

"I appreciate that," I say, "But the best way to protect me is to not let anyone see you. No matter what. Understand?"

He scowls.

"Tell me you understand the mission, Aries."

Irritation burns brightly in his eyes. "I understand the mission."

I turn for the door but not before he adds, "Unless your life is threatened, in which case, the mission will be to protect you at all costs."

I sigh. "It's going to be a long night."

The hallway outside my apartment leads straight to the elevator, but I bypass it and instead opt for the stairs. Part of me wants to take him for an elevator ride if only to introduce him to modern technology he may never experience again. But I can't risk us being spotted when we step off on the main floor, so stairs it is.

At the bottom, I pause, cracking open the stairwell door to peer out into the stacks. It opens to the shifter section, which is usually pretty quiet unless it's a full moon, which, thankfully, it's not. If it were, Bingo would be awake and prowling, and his nose wouldn't miss a damned dragon, either.

Behind me, Aries presses in close to peer over my head, and I suck in a sharp breath as I feel his hip bump mine.

Heat spreads through my body before I can focus on something—anything—else. Shit, I want to bump so much more than hips with this guy. Ugh.

"Coast is clear," I say and slip out into the dimly lit stacks.

With any luck, I'm right, and the coast is actually clear, but either way, at least I'm not about to back dat ass up. When this is over, I really need to work on self-control.

Maybe go on a non-fiction-only binge session. I think I saw a book about Manifesting your HEA in the non-fiction section. Yeah. Maybe I should give that a try. No sex books for at least a month as punishment for releasing and nearly mounting a dragon-god.

With Aries at my heels, I slip through the library, sticking to shadowed corners and remote routes. We pass an aisle producing overly loud snores from its shadows, and as we creep past, I spot Bingo curled up and sound asleep.

I move quickly past.

"What was that beast?" Aries whispers when we're clear.

"Bingo."

"And he's a...?"

"Hellhound."

Aries stops walking. I double back, impatient and terrified we'll be spotted.

"What?" I hiss.

"Hellhounds are a myth."

"Not here, they aren't. Though Bingo definitely knows he's one-of-a-kind. The little beast acts like he owns the place."

Aries just looks at me.

"Come on."

I lead the way, and thankfully, Aries starts moving again. Sconces glow from the far walls, plunging the center into near darkness. Not that it matters. Every creature in this place has supernatural senses including heightened eyesight. Still, no one knows this place better than I do, and for once, I'm grateful for a childhood spent among the lonely stacks of the Athenaeum.

We make it through the shifter section and then straight back to the reference area. Tables are set up in an open space to allow for the review and study of materials. This is where guests tend to spend the most time, but with the late hour, the space is empty, and the lights are off. We skirt past with no problem.

Up ahead, the path forks. To the right, a narrow spiral staircase leads up to the alchemy section. "That's where we'll go next," I whisper, pointing up at it. "First, we have to put this back," I add, taking his book out from underneath my arm. "Ready?"

He nods.

Shit. Here goes nothing.

I take the walkway to the left which circles around the outside of the aisles, running all the way from front to back. I know from our times patrolling together, Blossom will have kept to the inner aisles to cover more ground, so this is our best shot. It's also, technically, the most vulnerable option with no shelves for cover until we reach the winged creatures section. I don't bother mentioning that to Aries.

It's too late for second thoughts.

Halfway down, the back of my neck prickles, and I glance back. Aries meets my eyes, his brows dipping in silent question. My gaze darts past him, drawn to the second-floor landing where the alchemy section is swathed in heavy shadows. In the near-darkness, I swear something moves.

My foot catches, and I stumble, avoiding a face plant when Aries' strong hands pick me clear up off the ground. My head whips back around, and I meet Aries' wide-eyed stare, my chest heaving.

He sets me back on my feet, but his warm hands remain where they are, firmly planted low on my hips. It doesn't help my effort to breathe, but it damn sure feels delicious.

"You okay?" he asks in a low, rumbly voice I want to

bottle and sell to all the ASMR lovers in the world, then retire early.

"Yeah." My breath whooshes out on the word.

Aries looks skeptical, but he finally releases me. My hips tingle where he was just touching them. Something about his darkening expression tells me he knows exactly what his touch does to me too.

I clear my throat before remembering I'm supposed to be stealthy right now. Son of a ... I suck at ninja mode. "Come on."

We start again, thankfully reaching the winged creatures section with no more incidents. I count the aisles until I recognize the one from last night. The only evidence of what happened is a small coffee-colored stain that's barely noticeable, but still, I feel like there's some sort of neon banner blinking overhead to announce it.

At least there's no sign of Blossom.

"Okay, your book goes at the far end there," I whisper. "I'm going to run down and put it back."

Aries looks at me like I'm not to be trusted. "I wonder if I should be the one to do the running?"

"I tripped one time," I hiss then realize that's not exactly true. "Fine, two times. And one of those times, I unleashed a dragon, but that doesn't mean I can't do this."

"Of course," he says, his tone patronizing. "I only meant to help."

I scowl and turn around to face the aisle in question.

There and back. Quick and easy. Then we can go looking for answers.

I inhale a deep breath and then, slowly, blow it out again. With the book clutched in one hand, I bend my knees and pause, listening one last time to be sure we're alone. With only silence surrounding us, I take off.

My legs pump, and my sneakers hit the carpet with barely a sound. In half a dozen strides, I reach the end of the aisle, and my eyes find the small, almost imperceptible gap between volumes. Lining up the cover to the opening, I push the book into its rightful place and then turn and run back.

I almost make it, too.

Above our heads, I sense movement. The distraction is enough to make me stumble the last step. Aries throws his arms out to catch me, but the momentum throws him off balance, and he is driven backward until his shoulders bump into the wall. One of the sconces comes loose and falls. The carpet mutes the sound of the iron hitting the floor, but it's still plenty loud enough to bring a keeper running.

In a place where only silence and stillness should reign, even the slightest disturbance sounds like chaos.

"Shit," I hiss as Aries and I both straighten again.

"Maybe they won't—"

Aries stops short at the sound of heavy footfalls somewhere in the stacks. Blossom and her boots are unmistakable.

"We need to go," I whisper, "Now!"

I grab his hand and beeline back the way we came. When we hit the fork at the back, instead of going straight up the stairs to the alchemy section, I go right, heading directly for the stairwell.

Aries hesitates, pulling on our joined hands.

"There's no time," I insist. "The keeper will be here any moment."

"There's something up there," he says, and I'm shocked into momentary stillness.

"You saw it too?"

"I feel it," he replies, his tone still a million miles away from me.

Damn. Maybe some supernatural senses are better than others. Or maybe mine just sucked.

"It doesn't matter, we have to get out of sight," I tell him.

He hesitates, and I step closer. "Aries, I know you want to get home, but if we're found, neither of us is going anywhere except into extinction. I need you to trust me, okay?"

"Okay."

This time, when I tug on his calloused hand, he follows.

We're nearly to the stairwell when something crashes. I shriek, covering my hand with my mouth to muffle it as Aries yanks me against him. A second crash sounds, and I look over in time to see a light fixture shattering against the floor in the place where I'd just stood.

I look up, noting a shadow darting off among the rafters. The same shadow I saw before. Fear grips me then as I realize whatever I've been seeing tonight has also seen me. And Aries. And they've just let us know it too.

"Are you all right?"

Aries' deep voice rumbles through his chest and into mine. That's when I realize I'm still clinging to him like some kind of spider monkey.

"Yeah," I squeak, peeling myself away from him.

"You sure?" He looks at me with those serious eyes, and I melt a little.

"I'm sure. You?"

"Fine." He looks up, studying the rafters and remaining fixtures above us. I do the same, but whoever it is has gone.

The broken fixtures leave shards of glass and broken bulbs beneath our feet, so every step crunches, and the sound of it makes me wince. Someone's going to come to investigate any second now. In fact, a noise this loud is going to set off—

A loud alarm blares to life, followed by a booming dog bark, and I wince.

"Shit!"

The sound of my voice is lost beneath the sound of the alarms. For the first time since we crept into the library, Aries looks worried.

"Come on," I say, knowing he probably can't hear me over the alarm. Grabbing his arm, I lead him the few steps left to the stairwell door. Shoving through it, I step back to give him access, and when he's through, I follow quickly and then shove the door closed behind us.

Above us, the doorway to the second-floor access opens, and panic grips me. The only other creatures who use these stairs besides me are--

The gnomes! Their voices fill the stairwell as they head this way.

Aries looks like he might just stay and fight, but I know better. Grabbing him again, I propel him backward until we reach the alcove behind the stairs. I shove him into it, all the way until his back hits the wall, then cram myself in against him.

We're exposed as hell here. But there's nowhere else to go.

The voices become louder as the pitter-patter of little feet traipse down the stairs. Aries meets my eyes, and I give him a shake of my head to convey that, hell no, he is not fighting anyone.

I hold my finger to my lips so he'll keep quiet.

Then we wait.

A few seconds later, two male gnomes reach the last step, jumping to the floor. Ted and Zed; each dressed in black-on-black tactical wear I sewed for them myself. They race toward the door leading out to the library, Ted launching Zed into the air so that Zed is able to grab the doorknob and twist it. The door swings open, and Ted rushes to help Zed prop it open, which they're just barely able to do with both of their body weights combined.

On their heels, something black and furry leaps the last few stairs onto the floor and then bounds out into the library. Ted and Zed follow with small battle cries, and then the door swings shut behind them, leaving us alone in relative silence. Well, other than the muted sound of the alarm coming through the door.

Still, I don't breathe or move or think too hard about all the delicious male parts I'm pressed against while Aries and I wait to see if we'll be discovered. Finally, the alarm shuts off, and in the ensuing silence, I can hear Ted issuing orders to whoever else has gathered on the other side of the door.

"...Kitty and Ned are already checking the rafters," Ted says. "I'm going to meet up with them and see if they've found any sort of trail to follow."

"Fine. I'm going to track down the signature left from whatever portal they used to get in." *Blossom*. I wince at the lethal tone she uses. She's pissed. This is happening on her watch, which means she'll answer for it. And I hate that it's my fault.

"I'm going to guard the area," Zed offers, "Make sure whoever it is doesn't come back."

"Good, we'll reconvene in twenty," Ted says.

Then they're silent.

I tell myself that my hesitation is to ensure we're

alone. But really, the heat of my body pressed against Aries in the dark of the stairwell is so damned delicious that it actually pains me to move away from him.

Even though I know we have to get out of here. Blossom or the gnomes could walk in and see us at any moment.

Slowly, I peel myself away from Aries and motion for him to stay close as we both creep past the door and up the stairs. My heart pounds with the force of a drum, and I don't breathe fully until we're back inside my apartment.

The moment the door closes behind us, I head for my bedroom. Aries puts a hand out to stop me.

"What's wrong?" I ask. My first thought is that he's injured. He did pull me away from that light fixture. It could have hit him when it shattered, or—

"I know our worlds are vastly different," he says, interrupting my panic. "That's to be expected. But... was that a goblin riding on the back of a rodent of some kind?"

I scoff, completely offended. "He's a gnome. She's a raccoon," I say haughtily. "Oh, *and* her name is Kitty."

"Kitty," he repeats.

"Yes. She's a true warrior, for your information. Just like Ted, Zed, and Ned."

CHAPTER 10
PAIGE

Did I seriously just defend three gnomes and a raccoon to a dragon? Survey says yes. Yes, I did.

Hearing myself say it out loud does sort of remind me how weird my life is—even for a supernatural. I've never heard of raccoons being domesticated in any other world but this one. And Aries' expression makes it clear he hasn't heard of it either.

"True warriors?" he questions.

"Yes," I snap. "They protect the library."

"I see."

I narrow my gaze then shove my finger into his chest. "Listen here, asshole, you do not get to come into my world, my library, and start insulting my friends." Riding the adrenaline high from nearly dying, I glare up at him, preparing to throw down if it comes to it. Though, why

I'm pissed at Aries is beyond me. He's not the one who tried dropping a light fixture on my head.

Aries grips my wrist then pulls me forward until I'm a mere breath from him. "I meant no offense, Paige," he says in that gravelly voice of his.

Fucknugget. That voice. Like the velvet wrapping on decadent chocolate.

"Fine." I rip my wrist free and take a step back so his scent will stop invading my lungs. "We have bigger problems, anyway."

"Bigger problems?"

"You said you *felt* whatever was upstairs?"

A muscle in his strong jaw twitches. "Yes."

"Well, whatever it was nearly killed us." I drop down onto my couch and close my eyes. The seat dips with Aries' weight as he takes a seat beside me, though he doesn't say anything. "Along with that lovely twist of events, the chaos it rained down on us tonight will surely have everyone on high alert. Which is going to make part two of our plan immensely more difficult."

"You should have given me a weapon," he says. "I could have slayed the creature and saved you all this frustration."

"Oh, could you have?" I crack open one eye. "And how would you have managed that without being seen?"

Aries is frustrated. His expression is one of controlled anger. So controlled I can practically feel him vibrating with it. "I am not accustomed to being so damned helpless."

"Or being told what to do," I say, and his eyes narrow. Despite his irritation, my mood softens some. It's not his fault that he's here, it's mine. So whatever burden that mistake brings with it will be mine alone to carry. I blow out a breath, my misplaced anger deflating. "I'm sorry. I was just seriously hoping to get you home tonight."

Pushing to my feet, I make my way into the kitchen to grab a bottle of wine from above the fridge. After opening it, I pour two glasses then hand one to Aries and take my seat beside him again.

He sniffs the liquid. "Wine?" he questions.

"Yes. In this world, we drink when plans blow up in our faces."

"In my world, we do the same," he says then downs half the glass.

I stare, rapt, as he swallows the liquid. A small muscle at the base of his throat pulses, and my breath catches. How did I get so lucky—and so cursed?

He lowers the glass, and I look away, pretending I hadn't found a man's throat muscles sexy as hell. Again.

"Glad to hear some traditions are true in all worlds," I manage to say. Then I lean back and close my eyes, refocusing on the problem at hand. "What are we going to do?"

Someone raps on my door.

"Paige. Open up!" *Blossom.*

"Fuck a duck!" I whisper loudly as I jump to my feet. "Get in my bedroom! Quickly!"

Aries stands then hesitates. "Are you going to be safe?"

"Yes! For fucks sake, she's my friend. Just go!"

He turns and walks quickly toward my room, disappearing inside, though the door remains cracked.

"Paige? I know you're home. Open up, or I'm kicking it in!"

I take two deep breaths then set my wine down. "Coming!" Forcing a smile, I stride across the living room and pull the door open. On the other side, Blossom's cotton candy pink eyes are sharp as she studies me.

"What took you so long?" She breezes into my apartment, stopping just inside the door. Blossom's trained gaze travels around my space until it lands on my single glass of wine. I exhale quietly, relieved Aries thought to take his glass with him.

"I was in my bedroom. Is everything okay?"

"Not sure." She turns back to me. "We had a disturbance downstairs."

"Oh damn. Really? What kind of disturbance?" I'm a *terrible* liar. Always have been. But with Aries's life and my future on the line, I manage to conjure up a look I seriously hope conveys shock.

"Someone cut a chandelier down near the stairwell. Ted, Ned, and Zed are still looking for clues." She cocks her head to the side. "You sure you're okay? You've been up here the entire time?"

"Where else would I be?"

"Fair enough. I just wanted to make sure that whatever caused the disturbance is gone and not hiding up here."

"Just me." I force a smile even as the lie is toxic on my tongue. "Thank you for checking on me."

"Anytime. Can you come down and help me do a walk-through? We can cover more ground if it's the two of us. I called Mag, but he didn't answer. Fucker's probably drinking to avoid admitting what a disappointment his life has become."

"Sure. Let me just run to the bathroom. It's where I was headed when you knocked. Meet you downstairs in five?"

I'm about to shut the door when Blossom presses her hand to it. Her eyes narrow. "What's that smell?"

"Smell?" I swallow hard.

She sniffs then gives me a look that makes my heart trip over itself. "You have company in there?"

"What company would I possibly have? The only person I hang out with in this place is you."

She looks unconvinced, so I add, "The gnomes brought me this weird incense with my last supply order."

"Huh." She looks mildly placated.

"You're welcome to come in and see it, but didn't you need me to help you do that walk-through?"

There. The glint in her eyes shifts back to the problem at hand, and I know I've effectively distracted her. For now.

"I'll meet you downstairs, but hurry up. And watch your back."

"Will do." I shut the door behind her then turn around and nearly run smack dab into Aries' massive chest. "What the hell, Aries."

"You are not going out there." His tone is sharp and leaves no room for argument.

"Excuse me? You do not get to order me around." I take a step back and place both hands on my hips so I can glare up at him. Given our height difference, I have to crane my neck, but I manage.

His eyes are narrowed on me. Azure pools that I could drown in should I just allow myself to take the leap. "It is not safe. You're not leaving this apartment unaccompanied."

"And just what do you expect me to say to Blossom? 'Oh, sorry, B, my new dragon overlord has decided I'm not trustworthy enough to step foot outside of my house without him.' Yeah, that's going to go over real well." I shove past him and move into my bedroom. I don't have to turn around to know he followed me.

The hair on the back of my neck stands on end as every nerve in my body fires at once. He's directly behind me, his body so close I could lean back and rest against him.

"You could have died tonight."

"Yeah. And we will both die if I don't get my ass out there and look normal." I turn to face him. "Blossom has my back. Plus, the gnomes. Not to mention Bingo. Whatever is out there will be outnumbered."

Aries's nostrils flare, and he growls. Low and deep, it vibrates through me even though we're not touching. Heat pools between my legs, lust burning a hole through me.

"No."

"You don't get to tell me what to do, Aries. If I don't go down there, she's going to know something is up and come looking. Do you want her to find you? Want her to kill you before we have a chance to get you home? Because that is *exactly* what she will do."

"If my death means you survive, then I will gladly be that sacrifice."

I stare at him, trying to decipher whether he's serious. But one look at the blue flames burning in his gaze and I know he is. A dragon I've known barely a day is willing to die for me. A strange feeling ripples through me, settling in my chest before I can figure out what it is. Nor do I want to know. In fact, none of my feelings have any place here.

He's probably suffering from Stockholm Syndrome or some shit. Being confined to a tiny apartment cannot be easy for a beast used to flying free.

"For shit's sake." I pinch the bridge of my nose. "All

this broody book boyfriend energy needs to get packed away. I am not the person to use it on, Aries. You understand?"

"What's a book boyfriend?"

"Ugh, I am not explaining that." I meet his gaze then press my hand against his chest and shove him back a step. "I've been on my own for practically my entire life. I can take care of myself, and you being here does not change that."

He leans down, close enough I can make out flecks of gold in his eyes. "You're wrong, Paige. It *does* change that because I am the one you are risking your life for, and I am not okay with it."

"I let you out! It's my fault you're here!"

"You're wrong. Are you the path that led me to this world? Yes. But I do not believe in chance. I am meant to be here. Likely to save you from whatever seems to be trying to kill you."

"It was a distraction," I say, dismissing it. "I just happened to be in the way."

"You could not sense the being," he replies, tone deadly. "*Evil* radiated from it. You were very much the target. Why? I cannot know, but I do know that, had I not been there, you would have died."

Our gazes lock, the tension between us palpable. I'm frustrated, obviously, but more than that, I want desperately to kiss him again. To feel his hands on my body, his lips on mine.

I want it more than I've ever wanted anything in my life.

Which is precisely why I take a step back.

Aries does the same, resignation in his piercing blue eyes. "Fine. Go. But if something happens to you, I will tear this library to shreds, looking for the one who harmed you, consequences be damned."

Four hours of patrols with Blossom and we managed to find nothing noteworthy. No fingerprints, no lost shoe, no lingering magic.

Nothing.

I ride the elevator back to my apartment, my feet aching, exhaustion plaguing every single inch of my body. The apartment is quiet, but Aries is sitting on the couch when I push inside.

He breathes a sigh of relief then stands, scanning the length of me. "Anything?"

"No. Whoever was there is thorough in covering their tracks. They left nothing behind. Not even any traces of magic. Which there should have been if they'd arrived and left through a portal."

"A portal?"

"Similar to what you came through; like a doorway to all of the other worlds. It's the only way in or out of the Athenaeum, but outside of a book acting up"—I give him a pointed look—"only keepers can conjure a portal from inside the building."

"What about customers?" he asks. "Surely, you have others who come to use the library."

I cross to the kitchen and go to work, pouring myself a generous glass of wine. For a brief moment, I consider something stronger, but I can't afford to get wasted now. Not with everyone else on alert for intruders. "The library is very strict with who it allows inside. And besides, a customer can conjure their own portal from their own side if they're approved to visit, but a keeper has to be the one to send them back."

"So the intruder was assisted in escaping by a keeper?"

I shake my head. "That's the thing I don't get. A conjured portal leaves a magic signature behind. You can sense it long after it's been opened and closed. But there was no trace of any magic, let alone a portal."

"And this keeper who came to you for help," he says. "You trust her not to aid in attacking you?"

I turn, full glass of wine in hand, and fix him with a steady stare.

"Blossom is not a traitor," I say firmly.

He doesn't look convinced. On a sigh, I cross into the living room and drop down onto the couch so we're at eye level. "Look, she's had a rough time of it. She was orphaned young and the families that took her in over the years weren't kind to her status as a unicorn shifter. She was bullied and took a lot of shit from other kids too. Then, she finally found a way to portal to her home world, only to find it destroyed. When they caught up to her, she was charged with illegal portal conjuring and sent here to be a keeper as punishment."

"Guarding this place is considered punishment?"

"Believe me, it can feel like a prison," I tell him. Questions spark in his eyes, but I don't want to answer anything he might ask—not about me—so I hastily bring this back to Blossom. "My point is she's all about following the rules so she can do her time and get the hell out of here. That's why she wouldn't take Mag's shift the other night. And why I was alone in the library when you... She's my friend, but she would turn us in in a heartbeat if she knew—if only to keep from letting the blame fall on her."

Aries frowns but says nothing. I know he's trying to come up with another scenario or some other way an intruder could have gotten in—and, more importantly, out. Frankly, so am I. Because something was definitely after us tonight, and worse, now it knows about Aries, which makes it a greater threat than simply being a chandelier ninja. Until I know what or who has discovered our secret, we're not safe from anyone.

Not even Blossom.

I take a generous sip of my wine then stand and head for my bathroom. "I'm going to grab a shower."

"Shower?" His confusion is absolute—and adorable.

I forget all about chandeliers and portals for the moment, a smile spreading over my face. "Come here."

Aries follows me into my small bathroom. The space is tight, made more so by the massive dragon sharing it with me.

"If you loved the sink and baseball, prepare to be dazzled, my fire-breathing friend."

I lean forward and, with my free hand, turn the knob. Water cascades down into the porcelain tub. Aries stares at it like he's seeing a damned miracle. The awe in his expression has me smiling wider.

"Magnificent," he breathes. "It's your own personal waterfall."

"Basically," I agree. "Anyway, you wash yourself with it then turn the knob when you're done to shut it off. You can make it warm or hot, depending on your preference. Me? I'm going for 'melt the skin' temperature."

"Melt—why would you want to..." He trails off, brows scrunching as he looks down at me. "I assume you are making a joke."

"Yes, Aries, I am making a joke." I shake my head then give him a light shove out the door. "Now get out so I can get naked."

He actually pauses, and my breath catches as I realize the mental picture I've just painted for us both.

I almost hope he offers to help me undress.

But after another moment, he turns and leaves the room, shutting the door softly behind him.

I undress quickly then step beneath the hot spray. "Yes," I groan as I feel my muscles begin to loosen. Knowing Aries will want a shower, too, though, I wash my hair quickly so I don't take all the hot water.

I'm just hanging my loofah up when I turn around and catch sight of a shadow in the shape of a man looming on the other side of my shower curtain.

Panic grips me, and I scream. Scrambling to rip the curtain open, I slip and come crashing down—hard. My hip takes the brunt of my fall, hurting so badly my scream dies abruptly and my eyes begin to water. My elbow hits the side of the tub, sending stinging agony up into my shoulder. I do my best to ignore it, forcing my eyes to focus on the figure still lurking beyond the half-open curtain.

But before I can make it out, the shadow blurs away as my door is ripped open. Aries yanks open the shower curtain and scans the shower, eyes murderous. "What happened?"

"What the hell were you doing in here?" I demand, too hurt to care that I'm lying in a naked tangle of limbs before the dragon god himself.

"What are you talking about? You screamed."

"I screamed because you were lurking like a perv," I say, my voice shrill.

"What? Paige, I came in when you screamed." He reaches over and turns the water off. In that moment, I am all too aware of how naked—and awkward—I am.

"Towel!" I hiss in pain as I try to stand. Aries offers me the towel, keeping his gaze averted to my face. With one arm, I manage to half-ass wrap it around myself.

My legs are weak, my body on adrenaline overload. I put a hand on the tile to steady myself and step gingerly out of the tub. Aries backs away but only enough to give me space to stand. He watches me warily as if waiting for me to collapse. He's not far off the mark. I use the towel bar for support then usher him backward as I make my way out to my bedroom. Once there, my scattered brain slowly begins to form coherent thought.

"You're hurt," Aries says, watching me hobble across the carpet.

I don't bother to answer. I'm too busy replaying what he just said. "Wait. You came in after I screamed?" I question once I'm seated on the edge of the bed.

"Yes. Of course. You think I was in there while you were in your shower?" When I don't answer, his expression hardens, and I glimpse the battle-worthy warrior inside him. "I am not a man who steals glances," Aries says, haughty. I've offended him, great. "If I look upon a woman, it is with her permission, and every ounce of my attention is trained on what she's freely offering. When I look at your naked body, Paige, you'll know. And you will have asked for it."

I swallow hard. I believe him—of course. And if I weren't so damned shaken, I bet I'd be imagining all sorts of ways Aries could pin his full attention on me.

"What happened?" He kneels in front of me as the realization of what I just saw sets in.

"Something was in there with me," I tell him. "I saw a shadow."

"A shadow," he repeats.

"Yes, like the one I saw earlier. Downstairs in the library. But this one had more shape."

"And what shape was that?"

"Like a man."

Aries's gaze hardens even further. "Stay here." He moves into my bathroom, then my closet, before slipping out into the rest of the apartment.

I use his absence to slip underneath my sheets, using them to cover my body better than the towel could. It's not for Aries' sake but for my own sense of vulnerability. My mind is whirring.

Is it possible I'm seeing things? Or was there someone in my freaking bathroom? There was no portal, no swirling light, so how the hell did whoever it was manage to leave without Aries seeing him?

"No one is here." Aries sits beside me. "Can I check your arm?"

"Sure." I hiss through clenched teeth when he manipulates it around, but the pain fades away as soon as he lets it go. "It doesn't feel broken, and trust me, I've broken plenty of bones to know. But it is going to leave one hell of a bruise."

I snort. "You should see my hip."

The moment the words are out, I realize what I'm offering. But instead of accepting, Aries grunts and releases me.

"Someone was in there with me," I insist. "I saw him."

He nods. "I believe you."

I turn to him, eyes wide as true fear settles into my bones. "What the hell was it? There's no way it was human or ordinary supernatural. Not if it was able to just vanish before you walked in."

"I don't know, Paige," he says gravely. "But I do believe you are in very real danger."

CHAPTER 11
ARIES

The color has yet to return to Paige's cheeks, and I find myself desperate to make her feel safe again. The need to shield her is far stronger than it should be given that we just met.

But it's a siren's call that's impossible to ignore.

Rather than wait for her invitation, I walk to her dresser and begin opening the drawers.

"What are you doing?" she asks.

"Looking for something for you to sleep in."

I expect her to argue as that seems to be what she enjoys doing. So, when she simply sighs and says, "Oh," my concern for her grows. As does my anger. My rage over another being spying on her in such a delicate state has my jaw clenching as I struggle to rein in my beast.

He wants blood.

And as for most instances—Paige and the mate call aside—my dragon and I understand each other.

Finding only socks in the first drawer, I close it and open the second. There are swaths of fabric, and I pick through them, trying to identify if they're suitable for sleeping, when my hand brushes something hard. I pick it up and hold it out, too surprised for words at the sight of such a brutal weapon in the home of this gentle female.

"Is this…?" I eventually turn to where Paige sits on the bed and find her smirking.

"A flail? Yes, it is."

I examine the spiked head hanging from the wooden handle by the loose rope. "And have you used it?" I ask, looking for evidence left of such usage.

"A few times," she says smugly.

"Hmm." I sniff the spiked head. No blood. "Truly?" I ask.

She rolls her eyes and huffs out a breath. "Fine, I've … swung it ominously at a few goblins, all right? Blossom sent them back inside their book before I could do anything else."

"I see." I try not to laugh.

"I would have kicked their asses," she defends.

"I'm sure you would have."

"Don't patronize me, dragon. Someone just peeped on me in the shower. If ever there was a time for me to have a weapon in my pajama drawer, it's now." Her scowl is endearing. As is this formidable weapon in the possession of someone who could never hurt a fly. But I have the sense not to say any of that out loud.

Instead, I return the weapon to its hiding place.

"Third drawer," she says, guiding me to her sleeping attire at last.

I follow her instructions and open a drawer stocked to the brim with soft fabrics patterned with fuzzy animals. I sift through until my eyes land on a fabric printed with tiny baby dragons—which look nothing like the real thing, and yet...my heart swells.

"Here." I hand them to her, and her lips quirk in the barest hint of a smile.

"You would choose these," she says. But she takes the clothing I hand her, and I move for the door.

"Where are you going?" she asks, her voice pitching high with fear.

I turn back. "To give you some privacy."

She bites her lip, and my dick twitches at the way she looks up at me from lowered lashes. "Will you... stay? I don't want to be alone."

My cock and my heart both scream so loudly that I have no choice but to say, "Of course."

Instead of leaving, I turn around and face the wall. My dragon rages at that, but the gentlemanly behavior my mother has ingrained in me can do nothing else. I wait, arms crossed, while Paige dresses. My mind conjures images of her naked body, wet from the shower and trembling from fear.

I might have only been there to protect her, but now that the danger has passed, I can't help appreciating the mental images of her beautiful body as she'd stood before me. The swell of her breasts and those taut, pink nipples. What they'd be like to touch, to taste—

"Okay. All done."

Her voice snaps me out of my daydreaming, and I tuck my erection as best I can before facing her again. Her wet hair hangs over her shoulders, framing her face in a way that makes her seem both innocent and intimate. The clothing she wears is loose against her curvy frame, but I don't need tighter lines to notice where her breasts push against her shirt. My erection aches for release. I avert my eyes before it can drive me to take her right here in this room.

Paige slips beneath the covers, reminding me what I've just agreed to, and I try not to think about her warm body curled against mine in that soft bed.

"I'll sleep on the floor," I say, my voice strangely hoarse in my ears.

"What?" Paige sits up again, frowning. "No way. The bed is more than big enough for both of us. Even if you are twice the size of anyone else I know."

My dragon hums at her praise.

"I don't mind," I say.

"Aries." The way she says my name shatters my resolve. "Please. I'm not... I don't want to make you uncomfortable," she adds, "But having someone watch me in the shower is just…" She shudders, and my will to resist vanishes.

I pull my shirt off and let it drop to the floor.

"I won't let anything happen to you," I say, rounding the bed and stretching out next to her. My skin prickles where I can feel her gaze on me, but I don't look up as I lie beside her and prop an arm behind my head.

I'm careful to keep enough space between us, and I don't bother with the blankets. My dragon urges me to scoot closer, to curl around her, shielding her petite frame with mine, but Paige made it clear before that she doesn't want this.

And I *can't* want this.

No matter how badly my dragon does.

I wait while she settles in and don't bother to point out that she's left the light on. We both fall silent, and I listen for signs of her breathing more evenly as sleep takes her over. After several minutes, though, she shifts, rolling toward me in the soft light.

Her eyes are large and trusting as she looks up at where I've propped myself against her headboard.

"Will you tell me about your world?" she asks, startling me with the question.

"Why?" I ask.

"Honestly? I could use the distraction right now. But also because I've never been anywhere. For someone who lives her life buried in fiction, I want to know something real about somewhere other than here. Please?"

"You aren't allowed to leave?" I ask. She'd told me that when her world was destroyed, she was forced to remain behind. But I never thought that would mean she wasn't allowed to leave the confines of the library. It sounds like imprisonment.

"I've been a few places," she defends and then, more softly, adds, "But only to empty worlds."

"Empty?"

"No people around," she explains. "I've seen some gorgeous scenery. Breathtaking waterfalls, majestic mountains, sandy beaches. But… nothing inhabited."

"Why not?"

"Hoc says it's dangerous."

I wait, but she doesn't say more, so I decide to keep my opinions of this Hoc to myself—for now. Though, the imagery of him keeping her locked away here, high in this proverbial tower, ring far too close to fairy tales my mother used to read to me as bedtime stories.

Which begs the question. Is he truly her hero? Or a villain?

"What's it like where you're from?" she asks. "Do they have libraries?"

Her question makes me smile.

"Astronia is a vast and wild place," I say, letting my mind drift to the memory of my home—a comforting thought as I'm stuck in this tiny room unable to shift and feel the open skies beneath my wings.

"Wild as in barbarians roam and pillage?" she asks,

eyes wide.

"Some," I say gravely. "The biggest threat to my people is the horde who seek to overthrow us and rule the land with cruelty and brutality."

"What is the hoard?"

"An army of orcs whose land borders our own far to the north. They live beyond the mountains in mostly ice, and they want our land for their own. Unfortunately, they want to wipe out our people in order to have it."

"They sound lovely," she deadpans, and I smirk at the obvious sarcasm.

"Aside from the war overshadowing the lands, Astronia is lovely," I tell her. "So much green. Mountains taller than anything you've ever seen. And at the heart of it, my home, Nemos Castle."

She lifts her head off the pillow, eyes wide. "You live in a castle?"

"Well, technically, it belongs to my mother until I take the throne but—"

"*Throne*?" she squeaks, sitting up fully now. Her tangled, damp hair hangs in her face, but she shoves it back, staring at me in wary disbelief. "You never said anything about a throne."

Now, it's my turn to shrug. "You never asked."

"Sarcasm, hilarious," she drawls, and I grin, but she only narrows her eyes further. "What sort of throne are we talking?" she asks, and I wonder if her talents don't lie in interrogation rather than guarding these books.

Because when she looks at me like that, I'll happily tell her any secret she wishes to know.

Cut me open and spill my heart out, for this woman can have it.

"A king's throne," I say. "The one I will inherit when my time comes."

Her jaw drops. "Are you seriously telling me that I spilled my pumpkin spice latte and inadvertently freed the king of all dragons?"

"I'm not a king yet," I remind her, amused by the way her eyes have widened to saucers. She's clearly impressed by my title, and while the females at home annoy me with their adoration, Paige is different. My beast finds her awe very flattering. He wants her to think he's special. He wants her to like him too.

It's the most childish, ridiculous feeling I've ever felt —and I can't seem to make it stop.

"So, you're a prince," she breathes as if to herself.

"I am the eldest prince. The Nemos heir to the throne of Astronia." I try not to notice my chest puffing a little as I give her my full title. Paige simply gawks.

I wait, my dragon hoping for more compliments. Instead, she groans and drops her face into her hands.

"I can't believe this," she says, her words muffled by the fact that her palms are pressed to her lips.

"What's wrong?" I ask.

"This is horrible," she says and looks up again.

"That I'm the heir?"

"Yes," she insists as if I'm being slow. "You're not just an escapee from a story; you're the main character! The fucking hero of it all! If I fuck this up... No, not an option. I have to get you back before anyone realizes..."

"Paige," I say, watching as she spirals inward, muttering to herself words I don't understand about destruction and stupidity. "Paige," I say again. "Paige!"

"What?" She breaks off from her tirade, blinking at me impatiently.

"I have no idea what you're talking about," I say.

"Right." She sighs, but her expression tightens, and I know whatever she's about to tell me isn't going to be good news. "So, remember how I told you about a thing called the Extrication?"

"Yes. You said the escapees were hunted down and destroyed. That's why we have to lie low."

"Right. Well, what I didn't tell you is that it wasn't just my book that was destroyed. There were quite a few that suffered the same fate as mine."

"This is why the escapees were trapped here."

"You don't get it. As the main character of your story, your life, while here in the Athenaeum, is tied to the life of your book. To the life of your very world. The books, and the worlds inside them, were destroyed at the moment of the escapees' death."

She watches me, waiting for me to understand. I run her words through my mind again, and then it clicks. Her concern makes perfect sense. Perfect, horrific sense.

"If my book is destroyed, or if I am killed, my world perishes with me."

"Yes."

I can feel my dragon rising, ready to meet any and all threats with the flames of its wrath, but I force it back. This is no place for that kind of rage. Not with Paige staring at me with those round, innocent eyes and the walls of her tiny bedroom closing in on us both, and nothing has changed, anyway. My beast would protect Paige at the cost of its own life. I know it as well as I know my name.

She watches me, clearly waiting for a reaction.

"We'll need to be careful," I say finally and settle back against the headboard again.

"That's it?" she asks, still eyeing me. "That's all you have to say?"

"What else is there? I'm here now. The damage is done." She winces, and I regret my word choice immediately. "That's not what I meant."

"It should be," she says. "I really fucked up. I'm sorry. You're important in your world. I'm sure people are losing their minds looking for you right now."

"My mother, yes," I admit. "But only so she can parade another potential mate before me. Leo probably thinks I've run off and hidden from her attempts."

"Your mother is helping you look for a wife?"

"Against my better judgment, yes."

Her expression shifts into something I can't quite

read, her scent—though—*that* I understand perfectly. *Jealousy*. My beast hums at the thought. "And—how's that going?"

"Not well," I admit. "Every female she's brought has been excruciatingly wrong. Though, I understand my mother's determination. Without a mate, I can't take the throne."

"I see."

Her jealous scent intensifies, and I bite back a smug smile. Still, her eyes are strangely unreadable. I can't take it. I have to put her out of her misery.

"The last woman was a flamingo shifter. Arrogant to the core, her kind is."

"A flamingo?" Paige chokes on a laugh. "As in, pink bird with super long legs?"

I grin. "You have them here, too, then."

"Not the marrying kind, no. The flamingos here remain birds as far as I know."

"Well. Esma had a personality as ostentatious as her inner creature. She certainly believed she was worthy of being queen."

"After a title, then," she says sadly. "I imagine that gets difficult. Trying to find love when all anyone sees is the power."

"Exactly." I feel oddly honored that she understands. That somehow, this woman sees straight through to my soul.

"No matter, though. I'm sure my mother will switch

her focus to Leo in my absence; it's only fair that he suffer for a while instead."

"Leo is ...?"

"My younger brother. A thorn in my side at times, but I trust no one more." A smile graces my lips even as my insides churn with fear. What if I never get back? What if —somehow—my life ends in this library, and my entire family pays the price?

She cocks her head, studying me. "You sound close."

"We are."

"You miss them."

"I do. And I worry for my kingdom. Without a dragon on the throne, the hoard grows bolder in their attacks."

She lays a hand on my arm, and I nearly jolt at the unexpected touch. My flesh warms beneath her palm, a shiver of awareness spreading up my arm.

"We're going to find a way to get you home," she says solemnly.

Our eyes meet, and I inhale the scent of her arousal. My own desire flares immediately, and I find myself straining to go to her, to close the distance and kiss her until she can't remember why she stopped it before. I want to hear her moan my name, to beg me to touch her and to let herself touch me. Her scent tells me she wants it too, but she doesn't move closer.

Instead, she withdraws her hand and lies down, resettling herself beneath the covers with enough space between us to remind me of the boundary she's put there.

I exhale, my own need battling for control, but I force it aside. What she needs now is protection. And as long as my dragon draws breath, it has sworn to give it to her. I lie quietly, unsure what to think of all the problems that presents until, eventually, Paige's breaths slow and become even with sleep.

Long after she's nodded off, I remain awake and aware of the threat hanging over us now. The dark energy I sensed earlier worries me. It's like nothing I've ever encountered before, and if it truly is nothing more than a shadow, no weapons will work against it. Not a flail and not even a dragon. My beast huffs at that, but I ignore him, my thoughts inevitably drifting back to the sleeping woman beside me.

Her shoulders rise and fall with the steady breaths of sleep. Seeing her lying beside me does strange things to my head, and it hits me then:

The figure Paige saw earlier is nowhere near as dangerous as my feelings for the woman beside me.

What I feel for her is improbable.

Impossible, even.

We're from different worlds, different times, and yet my dragon calls to her as he would his mate. I'm not sure I have the strength to leave her behind when the time comes for me to return home,

Because, impossibilities aside, Paige is *mine.*

CHAPTER 12
PAIGE

Heat at my back draws me from sleep. I freeze. *Who the hell is in my bed with me??*—and then it comes flooding back.

A man-shaped shadow looming outside my shower.

Me falling—and hitting the side of the tub hard.

Aries coming to the rescue.

Aries. The future freaking king of Astronia.

He's solid behind me in bed. His massive arm is draped over my waist. I start to move, to try to get out from underneath him before my lust causes me to spontaneously combust, but he tightens his hold, pulling me back and pressing my ass directly against his *massive* arousal.

Holy shit. As if my initial perusal of his naked body hadn't convinced me...this does the trick. Paranormal romance novels got it right. Dragons are bigger —everywhere.

I stiffen, heat pooling between my legs until it threatens to consume me. The throbbing is next, and I clamp my legs together in an attempt to ease the ache.

I'm hyper-aware of Aries' hand resting against my hip. One brush over me and I'll be a goner. Which is why I stop moving. Because if he manages to give me an orgasm from just sleeping behind me, I'm not sure I'll want to return him.

Maybe I'll keep him chained to my bed. Just offer him a constant buffet of food and sex. Men like that, right?

He'll survive, and his brother can rule in his stead. Win-win? Even as I think it, guilt crushes me over my selfishness. *Get it together, Paige.*

Aries groans and grinds his erection into me.

"Aries?" I whisper.

Nothing.

His grip tightens.

"Aries?" I say, a little louder this time. Because as much as I would love to have him screw me into next week, it's just not a good idea. Not when our futures are absolutely headed in opposite directions. Opposite worlds, even.

But when he presses into me again, and my nipples harden, the fabric of my shirt scraping deliciously against them—"Aries!"

I all but scream his name now.

He freezes. Then rolls away me and out of the bed faster than I've ever seen a man move.

By the time I've rolled over to look at him, he's standing with his back to my wall, a tent in his low-slung sweatpants. I cannot help but let my gaze drop to it. I mean, I've already seen it, so imagining it now is relatively easy.

"If you keep looking at me like that, I don't know that I have the restraint to keep my hands off you." His voice is strained with tight control. I look up at him. His eyes are on fire. Brightly lit, much in the way they were that first night. "My dragon is quite—enamored—by you," he says slowly.

Every nerve ending in my body feels his words like a stroking to my senses. He wants me. As much as I want him. And while I'm thrilled by the knowledge, I am also very aware that wanting is as far as this can go.

Especially after what he told me last night. He can't rule his kingdom without his mate. And that, I am not.

I won't derail his future as king just for an orgasm. Not even a mind-bending, best-sex-of-your-life, come-and-combust orgasm. Ugh.

So, instead of letting my pleasure show at his words, I aim for casual.

"The feeling is mutual," I say as I scoot to the edge of the bed. He doesn't answer, and I purposely don't look over to see his expression. After swinging my legs over the edge, I yawn and stretch, wincing at the soreness in my hip and arm, then get to my feet and head into the bathroom. My limbs are stiff, and the bruise on my hip pulses with my movements. Today is going to suck.

As the bathroom looms closer, fear slams into me then, and I forget about Aries' impressive morning wood in favor of recalling the threat that made me ask him to be here in the first place.

The shower creeper. Suddenly, going into the bathroom doesn't seem like such an escape after all.

"Um. Can you stand out here? Just in case?"

He dips his head in a nod. "Of course."

"Great." I move into the bathroom, shut the door, then exhale heavily as I try to figure out how I'm going to let go of the man in the next room when I've only just found him.

"You stay up here. Understand? At *all* costs. Do not come downstairs unless the place is burning around you." I glare at Aries, hoping I'm coming through loud and clear, given that we've been arguing for the last thirty minutes about him coming with me to work.

He smirks. "I'm a dragon. Fire will not harm me even in my human form."

I roll my eyes. "Fine. Great. Then stay here even if the place burns to the ground."

His amusement vanishes as he asks, "How do you

know you'll be safe?"

"As I told you, the library is open today. It will be crawling with people. Nothing is going to be able to get me while the keepers are on high alert and monitoring everyone."

"The stranger managed to get in last night when the evening guards should have been on high alert. And someone got into your room last night without either of us knowing."

"Not a someone, a something," I correct.

"What?"

I sigh. "The thing I saw didn't have a corporeal form."

"You think it was a spirit of some kind?"

Shrugging, I consider. "I don't know what to think. The damn thing looked like Peter Pan's lost shadow to me."

"Peter who?"

"Ugh. Never mind." Pinching the bridge of my nose, I try to remember that it's my fault he's here, so dealing with his over-bearing book-boyfriend ass is on me. "I will be on the look for shadows looming around me, and I will be overly cautious of not being alone today. Deal?"

Aries narrows his gaze but nods.

"You be careful too. He was in this apartment," I remind him.

Aries grins though it's more of a show of teeth than amusement. "I hope this spirit shows up. Then I can deal with it myself, and you'll be safe."

"Do not tear up my apartment. TV and food. That's all," I say as I get a mental image of Aries wrestling with some unknown assailant. Honestly, the way his eyes glitter with the promise of pain leaves no doubt he can handle himself in a fight. But my heart apparently isn't convinced as it squeezes in sudden fear at something happening to him. "Deal?"

"Baseball and ale, all day," he assures me.

I shake my head. "Great. See you later." I step out of my apartment then shut the door and lock it. Then, I turn around and nearly run right into Hoc. "Shit! You scared me." I press a hand to my heart then remember the massive dragon standing on the other side of my door, and my panic only increases. "Good morning, Hoc."

"Good morning, Paige. I was just coming to see if we could have some coffee?" He gestures toward my apartment.

"Actually, I'm all out. Was headed downstairs to the break room for some." I link my arm through his and guide him away from my place—and the sexy as fuck fugitive it harbors. Walking without a limp proves harder than I'd hoped but Hoc's arm is the support I need to pull it off.

"I'm surprised you let yourself run out," he jokes. "You usually can't live without your morning coffee."

"With everything going on, I forgot to give the gnomes my grocery order this week."

Hoc and I make our way toward the elevator, and once inside, I release him.

"Yes, I heard of the issue last night," he says. "You saw no one?"

"Nope. We searched everywhere. Even had Bingo out looking. He couldn't catch a scent, and we didn't find a trace of magic or a portal."

"Hmm." He remains silent until the elevator doors open and we step out onto the library's main floor. It's empty, for now, as the first patrons won't be arriving for another half hour.

"It's troublesome that someone managed to get into the library without setting off the wards," Hoc says. "Magic is not typically cheated and especially the magic of the Athenaeum. Whomever has done so must be immensely powerful."

Or a shadow creature not solid enough to set off the ward alarms. "Do you have any ideas on who it could be?"

"Not yet, and until I do, I caution you to be wary. Watch out for yourself, Paige."

The way he says it makes the hairs on the back of my neck stand on end. Like he somehow knows that chandelier was meant for my head. "I hardly doubt whoever it is will pay any mind to me. I'm no one."

"You are a future keeper." Hoc stops walking, so I do the same and face him. He rests a large hand on my shoulder. "That makes you far more valuable than you realize."

I swallow hard. "Not as valuable as an actual keeper,

though. Blossom and Mag are at the top of that list."

He smiles in a tight line then releases my shoulder and reaches up to run a hand down his grey beard in the way he does when he's uncomfortable. Which doesn't happen often. "Blossom and Mag are able to protect themselves, Paige."

While true, his words sting. They're a massive blow to the ego, and frankly—piss me off. I've been protecting myself just fine, haven't I? Harboring a secret dragon upstairs and dealing with shadow men lurking in my shower.

Not that I can tell him either of those things.

"I'll be fine, Hoc," I assure him as my throat burns with raw emotion. I may not be a powerful supernatural like Blossom or Mag. Might not be able to fight or wield a sword, but I am *anything* but helpless.

I just wish everyone else could see it.

"Paige."

I look up as Blossom rounds the corner with a strange man beside her. Dressed in a light grey, pin-striped suit and fedora, he looks like a high roller who has just stepped straight out of a 'forties mobster movie.

He's handsome, despite being at least three decades older than me, and when he smiles, two dimples appear on either side of his full mouth.

"Hi." I glance between them. "Can I help you?"

"Mr. Morris needs help looking through some books in the alchemy section," Blossom explains. "He's writing an article on ancient magic."

I plaster on my best smile. "I can certainly help with that. Hi, I'm Paige, one of the librarians." He takes my outstretched hand.

"Morris, please," he says. "It is a pleasure to meet you, Paige."

"Likewise."

"Great." Blossom claps her hands together. "I'm off to do my rounds. You're in good hands, Mr. Morris."

"I can see that." He reaches up and removes his hat, exposing a head full of dark hair.

"The alchemy section is this way." I begin walking, and he falls into step beside me.

"Are you all right?"

His question startles me, and I duck my head as I realize he's noticed my limp. My hip hasn't stopped throbbing since I woke, though I've done my best to hide it in front of the others. "I'm fine. Just a nasty spill. Clumsy of me, really."

"Ah."

"So, you're writing an article?" I ask as we head for the stairs in the back.

"Yes, I'm interested in the ancient ways alchemy was used to enhance the abilities of powerful witches and warlocks."

"Sounds intriguing."

"Quite fascinating," he agrees.

"What publication are you writing it for? Maybe I know it."

He hesitates for a quick beat and then admits, "For now, this is a personal project. Back in my home world, magic has been in the open for quite some time. Nearly all humans have otherworldly abilities though the ancient way has been lost for quite some time. It is my intent to bring light to the way of our ancestors once again."

"A noble quest."

He beams at me, showing straight white teeth and those damned dimples again. "I believe so as well."

At the back of the library, I opt for the lift instead of the stairs. It's creaky as hell and sometimes makes me wonder if I'm about to plummet to my death, but it's a hell of a lot less painful for my battered hip.

I step into the vintage elevator then wait for Morris to join me before closing and latching the ornate iron gate. After pressing the *up* button, I wait for the grinding of gears as the elevator climbs to the second level.

When it comes to a stop, I open the grate and step off—my foot landing nearly right on top of Ted as he zips by in a clear hurry.

"Watch it!" he screeches, nothing more than a blur of blond hair and black, tactical clothing.

"You watch it," I reply, startled and then annoyed.

He stops and looks up, huffing at my tone. "We're

working."

"So am I," I counter. "And you're right underfoot."

The gnome glares at me then straightens his black beanie and moves on his way.

"That is an interesting creature," Morris comments.

"Yes. And they know it, which makes them quite arrogant, too. Right this way." I gesture toward a cabinet off to the left. "All of the books are on alphabetized cards. You can find them by looking up their shelf and reference number." To demonstrate, I open one of the drawers and reach in for the first card I see. "Both are listed right here at the bottom of each card."

He studies then nods. "Easy enough. Will you be staying up here?"

"Yes. Unfortunately, the alchemy section requires a keeper escort at all times."

There's that charming smile again. "Great. I was hoping you'd be around to keep me company."

My own enthusiasm at babysitting a library guest doesn't quite match his, but at least I'm not alone, and I did promise Aries I'd make sure of that.

"I've lived here at the library all my life, and while I'm not technically a full keeper yet, I will be at the end of the month." *If no one discovers the dragon in my apartment.*

"Must have been an exciting childhood. To grow up in a place filled with such knowledge."

"It really was."

He plucks out a card, holding it up. "Lucky number one," he says and then begins walking through the stacks in search of the book he's chosen.

I follow, doing my duty as keeper-in-training and making sure he stays away from the restricted section and takes no pictures of the pages. Though, given that it appears he's from an era before camera phones were a thing, I don't think I need to worry about that.

People come here from parallel timelines nearly as often as they arrive from places that are nothing like ours. Creatures, warlocks, witches...I've seen it all.

Well, I haven't *seen* it all. Not with my own two eyes. One day, maybe I'd take a portal to one of those places and never come back. Spend my life exploring far-off worlds rather than simply reading about them. I nearly snort at the thought of what Hoc would say if I told him I wanted to give up being a keeper and just portal jump from world to world instead.

What would Aries say?

As soon as I think it, I dismiss the thought. Even if he didn't think I was crazy, it's not like he could invite me home for a visit during my travels. He needs a mate. Someone to help him rule a kingdom. Someone that is absolutely not me.

Instead, I remain dutifully among the shelves, assisting Morris in his own endeavors--and putting my own dreams aside.

CHAPTER 13
PAIGE

By lunch, Morris has flashed enough charming smiles at me that his dimples have dimmed. I'm beginning to wonder what sort of world he comes from that he's so very clearly hitting on a girl half his age. But, at least, he seems content to waste away hours in the alchemy section, which means I have plenty of time to do my own research under the pretense of helping him with his.

Pouring over dusty tomes that haven't been cracked in ages, I look for a spell that will send Aries home. Even if the idea of doing so eats away at me.

There's nothing specifically related to opening portals, or at least not in a way that will break through the Athenaeum's massive defenses against it. From the sounds of it, the only way to conjure the portal we need is with the help of a keeper.

That means my only real option is sweet-talking either Blossom or Mag into doing me a favor so huge it could very well get us all thrown out and our memories wiped clean. If Hoc doesn't kill Aries first.

Either way, I can't imagine Blossom agreeing to help. Friendship or not, she hates her role here and refuses to do anything that might jeopardize her release.

Mag is too mysterious for me to assume anything. Although, he does owe me for covering for him the other night. And, this really is all his fault when you boil it down.

Had he not left me in charge, I never would have accidentally released the king of all dragons.

Even as I *consider* going to him, I hate myself for playing the blame game. This is one hundred percent a Paige fuck up. I mean, seriously, screwing shit up might as well be my calling card.

You need the world turned upside down? Give Paige a call! She can do it in ten minutes or less, or you get your money back!

Ugh. Now I'm annoying myself.

Morris passes on the offer to join me in the visitor's lounge for a quick meal, and secretly, I'm relieved. An hour away from his wide smiles and not-so-subtle winks sounds nice.

The pain in my side is a dull reminder of last night, and the 'better than Folgers' way I woke up this morning.

I reach up and rub it—then freeze when I see Blossom headed straight for me.

"You okay?" Blossom asks, frowning as I attempt to walk by her without grimacing.

"All good," I say.

"You sure? You look...pained."

"I fell in the damned shower," I admit quietly, and she just grins.

"Did you break a hip, old lady?"

"Very funny. I'm going to lunch."

"He's not done yet?" she asks, nodding at where Morris still prowls the stacks in search of his next resource.

"No, and he turned down lunch. He's apparently really dedicated to this mission of his."

She frowns. "See you in an hour." She glances past me to Morris and adds, "Don't be late. Dude gives me perv vibes."

Honestly, I can't disagree. Though I do find it humorous that a blade-wielding unicorn shifter such as herself is creeped out by anyone at all.

Mag walks out of the break room just as I start to walk in.

"Hey," I say, stepping back so we don't collide.

He glowers. "What?"

"Whoa, why are you looking at me like I ran over your puppy?"

He glances around and then says in a low voice, "Your

near-miss the other night was the first strike in a string of issues. Hoc is breathing down my fucking neck."

"Near miss?" I swallow hard, pretending like his words don't cause me panic. "I told you, a wyvern got sassy, and I put it in its place. That was it."

"Yeah, well, we haven't had a quiet night since and Hoc is up my ass for what he thinks started it all."

"Shit, Mag. I'm sorry. I promise, there was nothing—"

"Yeah, I know." He waves me off. "I'm just in a piss-poor mood. What's up? You want to cheer me up?"

His brow arches, and I watch in real-time as he goes from snarly to flirty in the blink of an eye.

"Honestly, the way you're able to transition from accusing me of screwing you to actually trying to screw me is impressive."

He smirks, clearly not understanding that by impressive I meant disgusting. "Is that a yes?"

Ugh. Clearly, now is not the time to ask for a favor. Not when he just clarified what his terms would be.

"Get out of my way, Mag. You're ruining my appetite."

"Speaking of appetite, have you seen Blossom?"

"She's babysitting a visitor in the alchemy section."

He starts to head that way, so I call out, "She's with a customer, you perv."

"I like an audience," he calls back and then disappears into the stacks.

I shuffle into the break room and go to work heating up my lunch, cursing my options for law-breaking keepers. Why can't a girl convince her co-workers to bend a rule now and then?

At quarter to five, lights flicker overhead, signaling closing time. Mr. Morris looks up from the large book he's been scouring for the last hour and blinks, bleary-eyed from the long day spent reading.

"Is that a signal of some kind?" he asks.

"It means we're closing in fifteen minutes," I tell him, stifling a yawn.

I haven't had a customer stay this long in ages. Between the stillness of this section and the ache in my hip, the idea of hauling my ass all the way up to my apartment right now is exhausting.

"Right. Apologies." He stands and grabs his jacket from where he draped it over the back of a chair earlier. "I shouldn't have forced you to sit with me for so long. Your injury..." He trails off as I stand, wincing.

"It's no problem," I say.

He starts to collect the books we've pulled, but I wave him off. "No need," I say. "We'll re-shelve them tonight into their proper place."

"I wonder if it would be easier to leave them since I'm planning to return tomorrow. I'd like to study this *Ancient Alchemy through the Ages* volume some more."

"Oh." My enthusiasm dims at the idea of being stuck

up here a second day in a row. "Even so, we're required to re-shelve nightly."

"I see. Well, then, Miss Paige, it's been a pleasure."

He lifts his hat in a farewell gesture before moving toward the stairs that will take him to the main floor.

"I can escort you back to the front," I say, but he's already descending the narrow staircase, his pace quicker than it's been all day.

"No need. I can see myself out," he calls back.

He's gone before I can respond.

I exhale heavily, limping slowly toward the elevator that will take me back down to the first floor where I'll simply cross to the west wall and ride another elevator right back up to my apartment. The stiffness in my muscles make it sound like a slog of a journey even though it's merely a few more steps before I'm home for the night.

Blossom is waiting for me on the first floor, her arms crossed as she studies me stepping off the vintage lift.

"That dude is creepy," she announces in a voice that has me shushing her in case he's still around.

"He's clearly from a much different world than ours," I say, not sure why I'm defending him. He *was* creepy. More times than not.

"Whatever." She rolls her eyes. "What's Mag's excuse then? He's creepy too."

I smile ruefully. "Unrequited love?"

She snorts. "No way. That asshole doesn't love. He lusts. Crudely and unashamedly."

"I heard my name." Mag steps out from the stacks like a jack-in-the-box, and I gasp.

Blossom glares at him. "Did you hear the part where I called you crude?"

"All I know is you're thinking about me when I'm not around." He smirks, and I glance between them, a plan forming.

A horrible fucking plan, but it's all I've got right now.

"You know... Blossom has a birthday coming up," I say, and Mag's eyes light with the information.

"What the hell," Blossom hisses at me. "That's not his business."

"Isn't it?" I ask innocently. "We work together, spend a lot of time together—I think that makes us friends."

Blossom's face flushes. She's going to kill me. But if this works...

"Anyway, we should all go out for a drink. Toast the birthday girl."

Blossom's anger turns smug as she says, "You know as well as I do that we're not allowed to socialize outside of work. Or have you forgotten the rules a keeper must follow?"

"Relax, I know a great little bar where no one would know us," I tell her.

"You know a bar?" Mag asks, and I school my features so he doesn't see my irritation at the jab.

"Just because I haven't been anywhere doesn't mean I don't hear things," I say. "There's this world called Astronia. It's without modern technology and untouched by the other worlds, meaning they can't detect keeper magic. We'd be flying under the radar the whole time."

"Astronia, huh?" Mag looks like he's actually considering it. "What do you say, Blossom? Birthday shots for the birthday girl? I might even luck out and get you in your birthday suit." He winks.

"I am not drinking with him," Blossom declares and stalks off.

My disappointment is nothing compared to what flashes in Mag's eyes before he schools his features. The look of hurt is gone so fast, but it's surprisingly real.

"I'll talk to her," I say.

"Don't bother." He slips back into the stacks without another sound.

Alone, I head upstairs, thoughts buzzing around my failed idea. If there is a way to convince them to open that portal, then there's also a chance I can get Aries through it too. No one will ever have to know about my mistake.

The problem is convincing Blossom to go anywhere with Mag. *Especially* on her birthday. But I've done harder things. Like resisting morning sex with the hot, well-endowed dragon king in my bed this morning.

If I can do that, I can do anything.

Right?

My apartment is quiet as I let myself in. It's also a complete mess. Bowls and cups are stacked and strewn across the coffee table. Hats and jackets from my hall closet are in heaps on the floor.

Annoyance burns through me as I follow the trail of items into my bedroom where I find even more mess.

My comforter is on the floor. The dresser has been cleared off, all its contents in small piles beside it. And the bookshelf I'd packed with romance novels is now empty. Instead, books are piled high along the wall beside it.

My eyes land on the bookshelf's angle and the way it's been pulled out from the wall. Directly above it, a chunk of ceiling is missing, leaving behind a gaping hole that leads to who-knows-where.

I have a feeling Aries knows where. Dammit.

Heart pounding, I cross the room and peer up into the darkness.

"Hello?"

No answer.

"Aries?"

There's shuffling from inside the ceiling, and then drywall rains down in dusty flakes as Aries appears through the hole.

"Paige, you're back."

"What the hell are you doing in the ceiling? And why does my apartment look like it was ransacked?"

He climbs down feet first, using the bookshelf for support before swinging himself easily to the floor. Then he smacks his hands to dust them off. His clothes—a pair of shorts that are oversized on me but way too tight on him, and a t-shirt that looks painted onto his large, muscled arms—are coated in dust.

Honestly, the thirst trap that is Aries, King of Dragons makes me care less about the mess in my apartment. I should be furious, but that fury makes way for heart-pounding lust.

Especially when he raises his blue gaze to mine. "I've been investigating all of the possible ways the intruder could have gotten in last night. I think I found something."

I stare at him. "You think whoever it was came in through the ceiling and then—what? Patched it up as he left?"

"Not exactly. There's a narrow passage behind your closet, did you know that?"

"Are you serious?"

"I'll show you." He leads me back to the entryway where a small coat closet stands beside my front door, and, sure enough, when he opens the closet door, the back wall is now a gaping hole.

"How did you find this?" I ask, staring in horror.

"My dragon can sense things like empty space." His expression darkens. "Especially if it feels confined."

Shit. His dragon is probably going crazy in this tiny-ass apartment. I hadn't even thought of that. Of how it must feel to be unable to access a part of you.

"This passage opening is cut directly into the wall with a door that slides free if you apply pressure here." He demonstrates and I watch as the door slides shut, looking like nothing more than the back wall of an old closet.

"Holy shit. I never knew," I say.

"With everything you had shoved in here, it was impossible to notice."

The jackets. Now I understand why they're littering my floor.

"Do you know where it leads?" I ask, fear lacing my tone. I shove it aside in favor of irritation at the mess. "And did you seriously have to destroy my apartment?"

"It was necessary," he replies quickly, though he doesn't bother to explain just *why* he needed to turn my entire place upside down when the empty space he sensed is in my closet. "And no idea where it leads yet. I didn't want to use this entrance in case someone else is monitoring the other end."

I cross my arms. "So, you made a hole in the ceiling instead?"

"I had hoped to catch a scent," he explains. "Something I can track. But there's nothing."

"Does that mean no one's used it?" I ask hopefully.

"That," he says slowly, "Or they're using magic to cover their tracks."

The weight of the day feels too heavy to hold up any longer. I sigh. “I need to sit.”

He rushes over and wraps an arm around my waist. “You’re in pain.” He guides me out into the living room, sets me on the couch, and helps me prop my feet up on the coffee table, then proceeds to hover like a worried mother. It’s adorable, though I don’t tell him that.

The relief at being off my feet—and hip—is enough to make me groan in appreciation.

“Not in pain anymore.” I offer a tight smile, but it only seems to make him more unhappy.

“Stay here.” He walks into the kitchen, and I listen as he rummages around. A moment later, he returns with a bottle of wine, a corkscrew, and a glass.

“You’ve made yourself at home,” I joke as he goes to work uncorking the bottle.

He looks up, and understanding dawns. His glance slides guiltily to the stacked dishes and cups then back to me. “Apologies for the mess, I... my beast... cataloging treasures calms him.”

He goes back to work on the wine bottle, but I reach over and grab his wrist, halting him.

The way he says it, the embarrassment on his face, has guilt over my initial reaction settling on my shoulders. I’ve expected this man—this dragon—to settle into a lifestyle that is not his own, in a world where he doesn’t belong.

“Aries,” I say, “You don’t have anything to be ashamed

of. Your dragon is welcome to do whatever he needs to feel comfortable here. I know he must hate being stuck like this."

"Thank you for understanding." Something flashes in his eyes, an emotion I don't expect and can't quite bring myself to name, and then he goes back to pouring the wine.

I let him, too exhausted from the day to try and decipher what just happened. Something tells me my acceptance of his weird dragon quirks has just earned me a new level of trust. I just have no idea what to do with it.

CHAPTER 14
PAIGE

The spray of the shower is hotter than I typically care for, but after a day like today, mind-numbing heat is exactly what I need. Already, the scalding water is loosening the stiffness in my body and draining the tension from walking on eggshells all day.

Speaking of heat. I can make out Aries' shadow in the gap between the floor and the bathroom door, lingering dutifully should my peeping tom show up again. My fingers tighten around the loofa as he shifts his weight, his back coming into view in the small opening I left.

He's mere feet away, shirtless, while I'm naked.

The thought brings a wave of lust burning through my veins as I imagine him opening the door and coming inside. I can picture it clearly, him pulling back the shower curtain and capturing my lips with his.

His hands on my body. His tongue in my mouth. My arousal is near-instant, and I clamp my thighs together to ease the throbbing. All it does, though, is make it worse.

What would he look like hot and soapy?

Cut it out, Paige.

But even as I try to shut it down—try to remind myself what's at stake if I don't send him away—I recall the way he felt pressed against my back this morning. The hardness of his arousal straining against me.

Desire pummels the walls I erected between us until only rubble remains. "Dammit." I shut the shower off and take a deep breath.

He's a dragon.

Not just any dragon, either. The king of dragons. In a world far from my own.

And he has to go home.

Or both of us might be killed.

"Paige? Are you all right?" his voice wraps around me like a thick blanket.

"I..." I climb out and dry off.

"Paige?" Aries calls out when I don't answer.

"Sorry. Yeah. Fine." But when I reach for my clothes—I realize with great frustration that they're not there. Shit. The shorts and tank I plan on wearing are still sitting nestled in my dresser drawers.

"Dammit, Paige," I murmur. With no other option, I secure the towel around my chest then push the door open.

Aries moves back until he's nearly on top of the bed.

His lips part slightly, his eyes burning with hunger.

"I forgot my clothes," I say, though the words are half-hearted at best.

Aries doesn't move.

Honestly, he could be made of stone for the way he stands there watching me. Frozen. Sculpted muscle on full display and freshly clean from the shower he took before me.

What would his flesh feel like beneath my fingertips?

My lips?

Aries's nostrils flare. "Paige." My name on his lips is a warning. "What are you thinking about?" He takes a step toward me, the look in his eye matching perfectly with the direction of my thoughts.

Startled, I throw up a hand. "No. You can't come any closer."

Aries stops, eyes narrowing. "Why not?"

"You know why. This—we—it would be a mistake. You're going home soon, and my place is here. In the library."

Ignoring my warning, Aries prowls forward, and my nipples strain beneath the towel at the way he looks at me. "Your arousal is driving me fucking wild," he growls, eyes flashing brightly with power. "I can sense it, and I want to fucking taste it."

"Yeah. Well. Your erection this morning was no help." I may be inexperienced, but I've read enough to know his was a hell of a lot larger than what's considered normal. Even by supernatural standards.

His gaze burns with challenge. "I want my hands on you."

My breath hitches.

"Want to hear you cry out as you come." Aries steps closer as the blood in my ears begins to thunder so loudly I can hardly think straight.

This is bad.

So, so, so bad.

And so freaking good.

Aries stops a few inches from me then reaches up and trails a finger along my jaw. I tilt my head, giving him access to my throat. "I haven't been able to forget the way you tasted." He leans in.

"I—we—this is bad, Aries."

"Is it?" he questions as he leans in, his breath hot on my flesh. The throbbing between my legs becomes unbearable.

One light breeze.

That's all it would take, and I'd come undone.

"You smell so fucking delectable." His lips trace over my jaw, searing my flesh in their wake. "Tell me to stop," he whispers. "I know you don't want me to, Paige. But if you ask, I will respect the lie."

"I—" My brain short circuits because what I *should* say is 'stop.' What comes out, though, is a defeated sigh before I cup his face with both hands and yank him down to me. I press my lips to his, pinning him against me as I feed the fire burning within me.

A fire that didn't exist until this dragon emerged from the pages.

Aries wraps his arms around me and lifts, crushing me against his body as his tongue plunges into my mouth. It slides against mine as he backs me up and presses me against the wall.

My hip aches in protest, but the ache is nothing compared to the desire burning me from the inside out. I want him. Want this. I've wanted it since the moment he showed up in the library.

Wet.

Naked.

Just like I am now.

My body comes to life in his hands as he reaches down and trails calloused palms beneath my towel and over my thighs. He grips my ass and lifts me off my feet.

I wrap my legs around his waist then bury my hands in his hair as he carries me. My mattress is soft beneath my back, his body hard at my front. The barrier of his shorts is too much, so I reach down between us with trembling fingers.

Aries pulls back and takes my hands. "Are you afraid?" he questions.

"I—Yes. I've never—" Embarrassment flushes my cheeks.

His eyes widen. "You've never been with a man?"

"No. Solo play only over here," I say then instantly wish I could disappear. Seriously. Can I not have one sexually tense moment where I don't put my foot in my mouth?

Aries is silent, so I try to wriggle away without losing the towel that's somehow still attached to my body. "Listen, I get it. I'm not experienced, you don't—"

In a blur of movement, he crushes his lips to mine, hands tightening around my wrists as his tongue dances with mine. Passion. Heat. It burns through me, incinerating my embarrassment.

"Will you let me be your first?" he whispers against my lips. "Let me show you how you deserve to be worshiped?"

I swallow hard. This is going to end horribly. But how many times does a girl get the opportunity to be ravished by the king of all book boyfriends? "Okay," I whisper.

Aries's smile is blinding. He grips the top of my towel and opens it. I close my eyes, and he growls. When I open my eyes again, I see that scales have appeared along his shoulders and upper arms. They gleam in the light, a shimmering obsidian that steals my breath.

"Fucking perfection." He leans down, and his scruff scrapes against my breast as his lips close around my nipple. I gasp. Wet heat scorches me as he draws the taut peak into his mouth. Pleasure unlike anything I've ever imagined possible shoots through my body like lightning.

Reflexively, I arch my back, desperate for more.

"Yes," I whisper, reaching up to run my hands over the scales still coating his shoulders. He shivers, barely suppressing a groan, and I revel in the power I hold over such a mighty creature.

Aries' hands slide down my body to my thighs. His lips trail down my body, over my belly, my hip, until he settles between my legs.

My breath catches in my chest when he looks up at me, eyes blazing blue fire. "I've dreamt of laying you out like this," he says quietly. "Of feasting on you until you come." His breath is hot against my core as the throbbing between my legs becomes unbearable.

I'm completely bare to him in a way I've never been to any man before, yet when he looks at me, I've never felt more confident. And when he leans down and runs his tongue over my clit, my release combusts.

"Yes," I scream, arching up as his mouth closes around me.

Aries moans, the hum of his low voice vibrating against my sensitive skin, and I see freaking stars.

I come undone.

Broken.

Shattered.

Even after I've lost it, Aries continues running his tongue over my clit. Sucking, tasting, *devouring,* until my second release builds. He slides that talented tongue inside of me, plunging it deep into my body and stroking the tender flesh inside.

I call out his name, "Aries!" as I come for the second time in as many minutes.

Seriously. His mouth must be magic.

Because never, in my entire life, have I *ever* felt like this.

"Please, Aries," I whisper. "I want to feel you."

In a blur, he climbs off the bed and shoves his pants down. His dick springs free, and my mouth goes dry. I knew it was huge.

Hell, I've seen proof of it for myself.

Felt it pressed against me.

But knowing where it's about to go—The mattress dips with his weight as he kneels between my legs.

"If it's too much, tell me," he says as he leans down and presses his lips to mine.

"O-okay," I stammer, my body trembling as his massive hand goes to my thigh and he positions himself at my entrance.

Aries's gaze locks on mine, and he presses slowly inside me.

The pain hits first. A stinging pressure that expands the more he fills me. I grip his biceps, squeezing as I struggle to breathe.

Aries stills inside of me, dropping his head down toward my throat. His breathing is ragged, his heart hammering so loudly even I can hear it.

"Are you okay?" he rasps.

"Yes."

He rocks against me, so slowly I can barely feel the thrust of his hips. Sensations pummel me. Pain then pleasure then pain again. After a moment, the pain begins to subside, making way for a feeling of pleasure and a sense of connection I've only ever dreamed of.

Then, he begins to move.

And pleasure takes over completely. A delicious friction that builds when he pulls back and reaches down to lift one of my legs up so he can get deeper.

"You're so fucking tight. So wet." Aries draws away then pushes back in, thrusting into me with a rhythm that matches the beating of my racing heart.

"Faster," I whisper, wanting more. All of him.

He increases the pace, and I wrap both legs around his waist, meeting him thrust for thrust. Our bodies entwined, our breathing little more than gasps of air, I hold on to Aries as another release consumes me.

Moaning his name, I come undone around him.

Aries pulls back and sits back on the bed, pumping himself in his hands until he comes and falls to his back, chest rising and falling rapidly. The scales on his arms recede until only muscled flesh remains.

It's not until I see the red tinge of my blood coating his dick that I realize we just had unprotected sex.

Shit.

"I'm so sorry. I should have—we should have used protection."

"I pulled out," he assures me as he sits up. "You will not get pregnant."

But the hollow look in his eyes makes me wonder if that doesn't bother him. Which, of course, makes no sense.

I close my eyes, feeling thoroughly and deliciously used.

The blankets shuffle as Aries gets out of bed. I hear the shower turn on but don't open my eyes. Unfamiliar emotions cloud my good mood.

What if he thinks it was a mistake?

What if I wasn't good enough?

What if—

"Come here."

I open my eyes to see Aries holding his arms out. "What? Why?"

"I'm going to clean you."

"Aries, that's really not—"

"Please do not deny me, Paige. I want to."

The idea of him washing me brings yet another wave of desire even as my body aches. But I sit up and swing my legs over the edge of the bed, anyway. "Okay."

Before I can stand, Aries scoops me up into his arms and carries me into the shower where he sets me carefully on my feet again. The spray is warm against my skin, and Aries wastes no time climbing in with me. He goes to work soaping up a fresh washcloth he must have already taken from the shelf by the shower and turning me so my back is against his chest.

"Your skin is so soft." He presses a kiss to the side of my neck as he reaches around and washes my breasts... my belly. Soft, even strokes that soothe me. "So smooth." Aries pulls away and washes my back then kneels before me and runs the loofa between my legs before washing them and then straightening before me.

He reaches just outside the curtain and grabs a second fresh washcloth from the stand directly beside my shower; then prepares to clean himself. I grip his wrist, stopping him.

"Can I?"

Aries nods and hands over the cloth. I start on his back, running the soapy square over his bunched muscles. Washing him is a new type of intimacy, and as I move around to his front, running the cloth over every inch of his body, I realize with great distress just how in over my head I am.

After tonight, my body belongs to Aries. How the hell am I supposed to let him go now?

MORNING COMES ALL TOO SOON. Testing with small movements, I note that my hip has already healed, and I'm grateful for my supernatural ability even if quick healing is all it affords me. No, this morning, I'm sore in another way; a delicious ache in my core that still doesn't ease the heat that encompasses me when I press back against Aries's naked body.

His arm tightens around my waist in response. "You think to torture me?" he asks as he presses his lips to the side of my throat.

"No torture," I whisper as I shiver in pleasure.

"Are you cold?"

"Not in the least," I reply.

He lifts his arm and pulls the covers off me then runs his fingertips down my side. "You are magnificent. The picture of perfection."

"I don't know about that," I laugh nervously.

"I do." Aries sits up and rolls me onto my back then positions himself between my legs, his hands on either side of my head. He leans down and captures my lips with his, a fiery kiss that speaks to the need in my veins. "How do you feel?"

"Like I had sex with a well-endowed dragon shifter last night?"

He grins. "Well-endowed?"

"I would say so."

Aries kisses me again then rolls onto his back. "Come here."

I roll over, expecting to curl into his side, but he shakes his head.

"I want you on my face."

"What?" Fear and excitement battle the desire in me.

"Now, Paige," he orders. "Or I'll punish you." The wicked smile that graces his face lets me know I'd likely enjoy every moment of said punishment. Still, I wouldn't want to disappoint him now, would I?

Nerves dancing in my belly, I climb up and straddle his face. Gripping the headboard for support, I close my eyes and hold my breath, but Aries orders, "Look at me."

So, I do.

I stare down at the man between my legs and hold my breath when he snakes both hands over my thighs and pulls me down on top of his mouth. I cry out as he pulls my clit into his mouth, sucking, tasting, devouring like he's a starving man.

Pleasure explodes through me, and I snake my fingers through my own hair, holding on while the orgasm rocks me.

"Aries," I whisper. "Please." I move my hips against his mouth. He grips my hips, holding me tightly to him as I come undone.

Stars explode in my vision, and it's all I can do to not scream his name from the damned rooftop.

Aries continues to draw out my pleasure until I'm completely and utterly sated, my body deliciously used. Then, I climb off his mouth and start to straddle his cock instead.

He chuckles and flips me onto my back. "You're not ready for round two just yet, love."

Love.

I know it's a pet name, a way to show appreciation for the time we've spent, but a selfish part of me wants it to mean more.

"I feel ready."

He covers my nipple with his lips then pulls away. "Tonight. You need a break, and I'm not sure I can be gentle now that I've had you."

His words only turn me on even further.

Rough? Yes, please.

At that exact moment, someone knocks on my front door, sending me into a panic.

"Shit," I hiss, scrambling to my feet. "Coming!"

Aries slaps my ass when I get up, and I turn to glare as he lies back on the bed, aroused and completely fucking naked. He flashes a self-satisfied grin at me that I plan to make him regret later.

Grabbing my robe as I go, I shut the door to my room and pull open the front door.

Blossom cocks her head to the side. "You're late."

"I am—" I trail off and check the clock. "Shit. I'm sorry. Overslept."

"Uh-huh." Her eyes narrow. "It smells like sex in here."

"How could it smell like sex? There's no one but me here. The Gnomes—"

"Bought you incense, yeah. That excuse worked last time. When I was already distracted." She crosses her arms. "Paige. How long have we known each other?"

"A long time," I admit.

"In all that time, you've never been late, and your apartment has never reeked of sex. Who's here?" Her eyes widen in horror. "Dear gods. Tell me it's not Mag."

"Ewww, no. I swear, it's not—"

The bedroom door opens, and Aries strolls out, wearing those damned sweatpants. *Fuck.* This is it. I've been made. Blossom is going to try to kill him; she's going to definitely kill me. I—

Blossom whistles, her gaze flicking from him to me and back to him again. "Nicely done, Paige. I approve. Incense my ass."

I don't know whether to laugh or hide. Aries comes up behind me and rests a hand on my shoulder. "I'm sorry I kept her."

"No," Blossom laughs, her sharp eyes taking him in all at once. "Do not apologize. I'm Paige's friend and co-worker, Blossom."

"Aries. Paige and I met a few days ago."

Blossom's eyes widen, and her grin spreads as she looks back at me again. "Well, as much as I hate to be a cock-block, you're needed downstairs. Hope to see you again, Aries."

"Likewise."

Blossom shoots me a smile that lets me know she will not be letting this go then walks off toward the elevator. As soon as I've shut the door, I turn and slam both hands into Aries's massive chest.

"What the hell are you doing?" I demand.

"She's a shifter," he replies. "Which means she could sense what we've done."

"Yeah, but you didn't have to show yourself! Don't you think she's going to wonder how you got in here without her opening a portal?1"

He chuckles. "Supernaturals come into this library all the time, do they not?"

"Yes. But only through the keeper portals."

"There is no way we could have met outside of here?"

"In the human world? I guess, but—"

"Then I am your lover. Your friend. And that's what she can know me as." He turns away as though this solves everything.

I groan and lean back against my door. Blossom is going to hammer me for details I can't give her.

Where did he come from?

How did we meet?

Somehow, I know, "from a book" and "naked in the flying creatures section" are not appropriate answers. Ugh. I am so completely and thoroughly fucked.

And the worst part is... I loved every minute of it.

CHAPTER 15
ARIES

I wait as long as I can after Paige leaves for work before making my own exit. She'll kill me if she finds out I've left, but my dragon is in no state to remain trapped inside this tiny living space any longer.

Not after last night.

It takes everything in me to keep from going with her to work—if only to reassure my beast that she's safe in that library without me. And since I know that won't go over nearly as well as my cataloging of her household items did, the only other option is to get some air.

I force myself to spend an hour cleaning up my mess from yesterday before giving in to my dragon's needs. When things are put right again, I shed my pants and prepare to slip away.

Pushing open the window beside the couch takes no effort at all. Fitting my large body through it, however, proves slightly more difficult. After some contorting, I manage to shove my body through.

Perched on the ledge, my scales already beginning to appear along my skin, I gaze at the world below me.

Large, four-wheeled machines snake past on the blackened earth. Glowing red lights wink from the backs of each one, and every so often, a loud foghorn sounds from several in a row.

"Traffic," Paige called it.

My dragon shudders at being stuck in such a tiny box. Worse than this apartment.

On either side of the traffic, humans make their way on foot. Even from way up here, I can see the pinched expressions they wear as they rush this way and that.

No one even looks up to notice a naked half-male, half-dragon clinging to the windowsill. Clearly, dragons aren't known in this world. Hopefully, I can keep it that way.

Satisfied it's safe, I crouch low and then shove off with legs that transform even as they propel me upward. My wings spring from my shoulders, extending and spreading until I catch the downdraft and use it to send me flying into the skies.

The wind is delicious against my scales.

My own weightlessness and sense of freedom up here in the wide open is heightened after days of confinement. Finally. My dragon can breathe up here.

And yet, with every mile I soar farther from Paige, the ache in my chest grows more painful.

I force myself to keep going, knowing the flight will do me good in the end. Besides, it's not like I can force my way into her workspace and have my way with her...

Though, the mental images of doing just that nearly send me into a head-on collision with a flock of geese.

Their cries alert me, and at the last second, I swerve wildly to avoid hitting the group, each one spread out from the other so that they form a "V" formation.

Speaking of V...

Knowing Paige's body has never belonged to anyone but me is something I can't forget. That she gave herself to me first—my dragon is way too fucking satisfied with himself over that one.

No matter how hard I try to distract myself, Paige consumes my thoughts. Her beauty, her responsiveness, her passion—everything about her is pure pleasure. I've wanted her since the moment I laid eyes on her that first night. And while my interest in her is not ideal for the situation, it's nothing compared to the recognition my dragon felt for her last night.

Despite the impossibility of it, my dragon is certain.

Paige Murphy is my true mate.

Not any of the women my mother has paraded before me. And not the maidens my brother has suggested I "sample" just to be sure.

It's Paige.

The absurdity of being yanked out of my own world and into this one only to find the woman I've searched my realms to find is almost humorous. Almost.

If I weren't faced with only two futures to choose from, neither of which offers a happy one.

My dragon balks at the thought.

To appease it, I swoop low, angling so that my wing trails over the surface of a pristine lake below. I've flown far from the city with only mountains and grassy valleys between them as far as my eye can see.

It's beautiful. But the ache in my chest is unbearable now, so I turn back again, climbing higher until the clouds swallow me up. If this is what it's like to be mere miles from my mate, stepping through a portal to another land without her beside me isn't even an option to consider.

I have to find another way.

PAIGE ARRIVES home looking more tired than usual. I hand her the wine I've already poured in anticipation of her arrival, and the smile she flashes me stirs my cock instantly. *Fuck, this is not the time.*

"You clearly know the way to my heart," she declares, sipping generously before making her way to the couch.

If only I did.

Instead of answering, I lower myself into the chair

beside her and wait, trying to come up with the right words to test my plan.

Paige sips her drink, oblivious to my struggle. "Oh, hey, you cleaned up," she remarks, glancing around the room. "Thank you."

I grunt an acknowledgment of her words, distracted. Finally, she notices my silence and peers at me over the rim of her glass.

"What's wrong?" she asks, worry pinching her features as she glances toward the closet. "Did you find another stalker tunnel?" She leans forward, suddenly stricken. "Did that shadow asshole return?"

"No," I assure her, "Nothing like that.

"Then what is it?"

"My dragon has been tense," I admit.

"Shit, Aries, I'm sorry. I can't imagine how hard this must be for you being cooped up in here." Her compassion transforms into hesitation. "I guess we should try to do some sleuthing tonight. See if we can find the spell that will open that portal for you. Though, I did spend two days scouring the alchemy section and found nothing. But hey, we can try the reference section next."

"Yes," I say, ignoring the tightness in my chest and putting aside my own agenda. "We probably should."

She downs her wine and stands.

"Should we wait for the others to go home?" I ask.

"Mag and Blossom already have. The gnomes are on duty tonight," she explains, walking to the kitchen and returning a moment later with a bag of something called Sour Patch. She holds it up and adds, "This will distract them so we can get into the reference section unseen."

I can't help my skepticism, but Paige seems certain of her prediction, so I follow her out and down the stairs. When we arrive on the first floor, I slip in front of her, stopping her from exiting the stairwell.

"What is it?" she asks, startled.

"I want to make sure it's clear." My dragon needs it, actually, but I don't tell her that. Nor do I tell her we're past the point of non-violence when it comes to protecting her. My dragon will kill anything that moves against his mate, no question.

Hopefully, it won't come to that, but if it does, I'll take the consequences willingly if it means keeping her safe.

She sighs but steps back, letting me ease the door open just far enough to sniff the air inside the library. I recognize the others: Blossom, Hoc, and a scent I've come to know as the other keeper Paige has told me about, Mag.

I also recognize the little men and their domesticated rodent from the other night. Their scents are strong as if they've come through here recently. Listening intently, I try to pick up their location among the quiet shelves.

Instead, what I find is another presence.

Too large to be a gnome or a rodent. And somehow, threatening.

When I sense movement, I react instantly. Yanking

the door closed, I lift Paige off her feet and carry her to the back of the stairs, pressing her into the small alcove where we hid once before.

She tries to protest, but I press my hand to her mouth, silencing her with a look.

She stares up at me with rounded eyes. I hold her gaze, all my senses trained toward the library. Something pauses on the other side of the door.

In the silence, the handle clicks as it moves.

The door creaks open, and the familiar evil scent slams into me.

The stranger from Paige's bathroom.

A figure moves into the open doorway. No, not a figure, I realize as I watch it enter the stairwell. A shadow.

Paige goes still. Fear rolls off her now.

My scales rush to the surface of my skin. My dragon wants blood, though I'm not sure there's any to spill from a phantom creature like this one.

And I can't risk Paige until I know for sure how to kill the threat.

Hating my options, I press Paige against the wall, covering her with my body, and wait.

Slowly, the shadow drifts through the doorway and up the stairs. The door clicks quietly shut behind it. I breathe silently, using its scent to track its progress. Up and up it goes.

Straight to the second floor. The door opens there too,

and I listen as the shadow passes into the hall, letting the door click shut again in its wake.

Finally, we're alone again.

Not that having the damned thing upstairs is any better.

Paige reaches up and pulls my hand from her mouth, her hand trembling. "It's going to my apartment," she whispers.

"It is," I agree grimly, my muscles straining with the need to go after it.

I step away before I've realized it, and Paige tightens her grip on my hand, pulling me back. "Don't leave me," she says.

I grimace. If she'd asked me not to hurt it, I would have refused. But asking me to protect her, to make her feel safe? I can't refuse that.

My shoulders sag as I realize I've been defeated. "Where else can we go?" I ask her.

She bites her lip, drawing my attention to her perfect mouth. "There's a basement," she says at last. "Warded against any creatures other than those sworn to the Athenaeum." At my expression, she adds, "I can get you in."

"Paige, wait," I say when she starts to move.

"Is something wrong?"

"No, I just... would you come with me to Astronia?" The words are rushed and clumsy. I grimace, kicking myself for the awkward delivery. I haven't felt this uncertain around a woman in, well, ever.

"Come with you?" she repeats, uncertainty reflected in her depthless eyes. "Why?"

"To see my world for yourself," I say lamely. "You enjoyed the description so much, and I know you'd love it even more if you saw it for yourself. This time of year, the trees are beginning to bud and bloom. The rivers are fast and flowing. And the forest animals are just beginning to emerge with their young. We could hike, or I could fly you to the perfect viewpoint to take it all in."

"It sounds perfect," she says, and my heart lifts with hope. "But also kind of impossible." Just as fast, hope crumbles.

"Impossible?" I repeat, disappointment igniting my temper. "Even with everything in this damned library trying to kill you?"

"Not everything," she argues.

"Right. Just a shadow creature stalking you in the shower. And unknown monsters constantly attempting to escape the confines of their literary cell. Not to mention whatever's climbing through that hidden passageway."

"Hey, you were an unknown monster until very recently," she points out.

I scowl. "And the rest?"

"None of it happened until you came along," she says, and I blink, taken aback. "Sorry," she says. "That's not what I meant."

I don't answer.

“Look, maybe I could swing a vacation once my internship ends,” she says, “but after that… I’ve sworn an oath to this place.”

Her words only serve to pain me even more. “What kind of oath?”

“The kind that binds me to the Athenaeum for life,” she says softly. “A promise to protect it for as long as I shall live.”

Her expression is soft as she says the words, and I wonder if she’s figured out my true motive for asking. But her oath is the same one I’ve sworn to my own kingdom. A promise to protect it, to rule as king, for as long as I live.

And so, I keep my secret. Because the only thing that comes close to the pain of losing Paige is hurting her. I won’t do either if I can help it.

I, however, am not so lucky as to be spared suffering. The future I want with Paige is more than impossible; it’s futile. And the pain of knowing it is worse than any death or confinement, in this world or the next.

CHAPTER 16
PAIGE

With the gnomes distracted by the pile of Sour Patch I left near the stairs and the shadow creature likely looting my apartment, I stroll through the shelves of the reference section.

So far, our search has turned up nothing.

No way of opening a book and sending him home. Likely because opening the books is strictly forbidden. Given that's literally rule number one, of course there wouldn't be a how-to recipe for breaking it. Not without a keeper to open a portal instead. And instructions for how to wield keeper magic aren't something recorded in any book. The library's language of magic is a mystery to anyone but the keepers themselves.

So, with that, we're literally back at square one.

Perfect.

I shut the cover of the tome in my hands and re-shelve it. Then, I glance over to where Aries looms between the stacks, his back to me. He's so large that he nearly blocks the entire gap, which is where he's remained since the moment we got here.

He'd been pissed about coming to this section at all. Had wanted to go straight to where I'd be safe.

But we have a mission. A job to do.

And as badly as I wish he could stay and we could keep playing house, the king of dragons belongs on his throne.

"Would you come with me to Astronia?" His offer lingers in my mind, and even as I know it's impossible, that doing so would put everything I've worked for in jeopardy, I'd be lying to myself if I didn't admit that there's a part of me intrigued at seeing the world that shaped such a man.

To witness him in his own natural territory. But remaining there isn't an option for me, and I have a feeling that once I ventured into his domain, I'd never want to leave.

Never want to abandon the man who has become my very reason for getting out of bed in the morning. As pathetic as that sounds given that we've only known each other less than a handful of days. But something about the way he looks at me suggests he feels the same.

That's what scares me most of all.

As if he can read my thoughts, Aries turns to me, blue gaze locking with mine and stealing my breath. The man standing before me is everything I would have wanted in a partner. In a man to spend my life with during those moments when I allowed myself to dream of such impossibilities.

And I can't have him.

"Anything?" he whispers.

I shake my head. "We'd better get going. The gnomes will likely be polishing off that bag soon."

He nods and reaches for my hand. I thread my fingers through his and ignore the strength his touch gives me.

"We can try to go back to my apartment—"

"No. I will go tomorrow when I know you're safe."

"Aries—"

"Don't ask me to put you at risk, Paige," he growls, eyes flashing. "It won't end well."

I swallow hard...but nod. Something in his tone has shifted since we left my apartment. I tell myself it's his dragon. That he doesn't like to be caged, but I also wonder if that's only part of it.

Does he want to return home more than he wants to be with me? Has he grown tired of me already?

"This way." I pull him toward the right where we can skirt the edges of the sections on our way to the basement access door. As we walk, I scan for the gnomes.

Thankfully, I still haven't seen any sign that my distraction didn't work. Little adorable bastards are predictable as can be with their candy addiction.

Finally, we arrive at a steel door labeled *Staff Only*. I

press my palm to the door and listen for the soft click of the wards disengaging.

As soon as they do, I turn back to Aries. "I need you close to me. So close we might as well be the same person. So the magic only reads one source of body heat."

With glittering eyes, Aries moves in and snakes an arm around my waist to yank me back against him. The breath leaves my lungs in a whoosh, and even though I know it's the last thing I should be at the moment, I'm turned the hell on.

"Like this?" he asks, breath against my cheek.

Ugh, the asshole knows exactly what he's doing right now.

"Yup. This should work." I shove the door open and start to walk, but our progress is clumsy thanks to our closeness. A problem that is immediately remedied when Aries lifts me into his arms instead.

I gasp and look up at him then immediately wish I hadn't. The air between us crackles with tension, and I forget why he's holding me in the first place.

Danger.

Yes, that's it.

Not sex.

Focus, Paige.

"Um. We should keep moving," I manage to say. Aries nods, but the look he gives me says he knows exactly what I'm thinking now.

We make it through the door, which closes and seals

behind us, then down the first set of stairs. At the landing, I stop and give the password that will allow us passage. "Custos."

I motion for Aries to continue down the next flight of stairs. My skin prickles with awareness as the magical alarm system fades behind us. "You can put me down now," I say.

He grunts and does.

Together, we descend the rest of the stairs. At the bottom, I reach up and click on the light, illuminating the empty space next to the furnace that's just large enough to hold roughly two school buses side-by-side.

It's empty now, though usually, it's used as a time-out for trouble-making books.

Which, given Aries, seems a perfect fit.

My nose wrinkles as the mildewy smell hits me. When I look over at Aries, I can tell he's less than impressed.

"This is where you wish to spend the night?" he asks.

"No. I want to be in my bed, but you said we couldn't go check my apartment."

"I will go check, just say the word."

"That's not what I meant."

"You are welcome to alert the others and have them search upstairs instead."

"You already know why I can't do that."

"And you already know how I feel about letting you

back upstairs tonight." Aries narrows his gaze on me. "I will not put you at risk."

"It's my life, though. My choice," I argue. "Just because we slept together—"

Aries closes the distance and yanks me against him, his lips brushing against my cheek. "You and I having sex absolutely changed things, Paige. There's no use denying it. And I will protect you with my last breath."

I swallow hard. What the hell am I supposed to say to that?

"Aries." I tilt my face up to look at him, trying my best to hide my anguish at what I'm about to say. "We can't ever be anything else."

His gaze darkens. "I know that."

"Then maybe we should—" He cuts me off by covering my mouth with his. His lips move against me, his tongue sliding over the seam of mine so I'll open for him.

Which I do, without hesitation.

I sink into the kiss, my hands sliding up his arms and into his hair. I hold onto the thick strands, pulling him closer as my entire body turns liquid in his hands.

Aries reaches down and lifts me then steps up toward the wall and presses me against it, his lips never leaving mine. I wrap both legs around his waist and hold him against me, his hard length pressing directly between my legs.

I moan against him, the pressure damn near too much.

I'm still sore from last night, but the idea of asking him to stop doesn't even cross my mind. We may not be able to be anything more than what we are right now, but what we are is pretty damned great, and I'd be a fool to waste even a moment of it.

So, I let my hands trail down and grip the bottom of his shirt. I rip it over his head and toss it to the ground then pull myself closer to him, his flesh hot against me.

Around us, the dingy basement fades away, taking every single one of our problems with it.

All that matters is him and me.

And the fiery passion between us.

I unhook my legs, and Aries sets me down. He pulls away, releasing my mouth to rest his forehead against mine. Then he lets out a hot breath that fans my face and slides down my body, kneeling at my feet.

His capable fingers toy with the button of my pants.

He opens them and slides them down my legs, the tips of his fingers grazing every inch of my flesh as he does. Within seconds, I'm standing before him in my shirt and lace underwear.

"You are perfection, Paige." Gripping my hips, he leans in and presses his lips to the tender flesh just above my underwear.

"You're not too bad yourself," I whisper, damn near breathless.

Aries grins up at me then lifts one of my legs and sets my foot on his shoulder to open me up. He leans in and runs his tongue over the barrier of my panties.

I gasp, my leg nearly buckling.

Then, he torments me further by looping a finger beneath the lace and pulling it to the side so he can run his tongue over my bare flesh.

"Yes," I whisper.

He draws my clit into his mouth and sucks tenderly, sending pleasure surging through my veins like a tsunami. I ache for him.

Burn for him.

"You taste so fucking good," he growls against me.

"I want you," I whisper. "Please."

Aries runs his tongue over me again then drives it into me.

"Oh!" I cry out as my release overtakes every single one of my senses. Fingers threading through his hair, I hold him against me as he continues sucking on the sensitive bud. He nips, reaching up to fill me with his finger.

The pressure is all-consuming.

The feel of him damn near too much for me to handle.

And then he's gone.

He sets my foot back down and stands then shoves his pants down. I do the same with my panties then rip my shirt over my head just in time for Aries to snake a hand around the back of my neck to pull me against him. He takes my mouth in a passionate frenzy of tongue and teeth.

With one hand on my ass, he lifts me, pinning me back against the wall and stepping between my legs. Then, he drives up into me.

"Yes!" I cry out as he begins to move.

In and out.

Thrusting as he fills me completely.

Last night was tender.

But tonight? Tonight, Aries fucks me with a furious passion.

He slams into me over and over again until my entire body comes apart. I clench around him and cry out, "Aries!" He doesn't let up.

Even when my orgasm sends me soaring straight up and out of this basement, Aries continues driving into me.

Then, he sets me down and pulls out, only to pump his dick until his release breaks through. He sucks in breath after breath, chest rising and falling in rapid succession so that it's nearly a direct match for my own.

"Did I hurt you?" he questions then reaches down and lifts his shirt to clean first me and then himself.

"No," I reply. "Are you okay?"

Aries smiles at me. "More than."

I return the gesture and then lean back against the cool wall. Without his body on mine, the cold seeps in, and I shiver. "I didn't really think this through," I say, laughing nervously. "It's pretty damn cold."

A muscle in his jaw flexes, and he eyes the stairs. "We will not be disturbed down here?"

I shake my head. "No one ever comes down here anymore."

He nods then tosses his shirt to the side. "Stand back."

"What are you going to do?"

"Shift."

"Into your dragon form?" I nearly choke out.

"Yes. My dragon runs hot. He can keep you warm."

"But—he's a dragon."

Aries grins. "Who is just as fascinated by you as I am. He will not hurt you."

I swallow hard. The chance to see a real dragon? Why the hell am I hesitating? "Go for it."

Aries closes his eyes and holds both arms out. Less than a heartbeat later, his flesh begins to transform, skin morphing to scales. Then, his entire body begins to change.

The cracking of bones fills the basement as his limbs and torso bend and break. My stomach churns, and I watch him, worried for what must be pain on his part, but the shift only lasts seconds.

And soon, he's filling the entire basement, a massive winged creature with obsidian scales that glimmer beneath the faint overhead light.

Holy shit. If the man steals my breath...this is life-changing. Soul-morphing. I'm standing before a dragon. No, not just any dragon. A king.

The massive animal drops his head and snorts.

I reach out with my hand, and he presses his large snout against it. His scales are rough and warm to the touch.

"Hi," I whisper. "You are magnificent." I let my hand trail up over his large head, down his muscled shoulder, until I reach leathery wings. They're smooth beneath my fingers, and I swear I hear the dragon groan when I caress them.

Seeing him this way, knowing this beast has been trapped inside of Aries, makes me feel even worse.

How much pain must he be in to only exist as half of himself?

"We'll get you home," I promise him. "Soon."

He glances back at me, huge blue eyes—the same shade as human Aries—unblinking. Then he lies on the concrete and extends his wing up. I cross over and settle on top of his leg as he curls his wing around me, tucking my body against his own.

In seconds, the chill is gone, leaving me feeling warm and safe.

So here, in the basement of the Athenaeum, in the arms of a dragon, I drift to sleep.

CHAPTER 17

ARIES

Paige's breathing quiets, and her body relaxes against my scales. I listen, counting her heartbeats to soothe my beast, who's not exactly thrilled with his sleeping arrangements for the night. The confinement is getting to him.

Still, at least I'm able to shift down here.

Nearby, heat emanates from a large machine of some kind. It emits a soft buzzing that, even after days of being in this world, still sounds like a roar in my ears.

My heart aches for home.

For the soft breezes that move our grasses.

For the bubbling brooks that bring fresh water to our homes.

But mostly, it aches for the chance to take the woman I love somewhere safe and familiar. Somewhere nothing and no one can ever harm her.

This world is loud and dangerous.

Toxic.

I don't belong in it—but Paige does.

Since the moment she told me of her vow to this place, I've thought of nothing else. And at the height of my desperation for her, our future became clear to me.

Her heart owns me whether she knows it or not.

There is no choice for me anymore.

I will stay with her, no matter what it costs me. To leave will kill me, but it's not my life I care about anymore. All that matters is the safety of my mate, and to ensure that, I must remain by her side to protect her from any threats that rise against her.

In order to do that, I must give up my kingdom. Something I *never* thought I would do. But for a lifetime with Paige?

There is nothing I won't do.

CHAPTER 18
PAIGE

My muscles protest the moment I try to move. When my eyes open, the light is soft—until I blink and realize there's a leathery wing blocking the harsh overhead lighting from my sleepy eyes.

"Ugh," I groan, blinking as the wing moves aside. I sit up, eyeing the dank basement around me with disdain.

Then, my eyes meet that of the dragon currently looking down at me, and my cheeks flush. I'm still naked. And very, very cuddly with a scaly beast.

"Your scales are softer than I imagined," I say before I can stop myself.

Those giant crystal eyes blink owlishly back at me.

Tentatively, I reach out and press my palm to the side of his face. Hot breath rushes from its nostrils, and I jerk my hand back.

The dragon ducks its head.

Is he...sorry?

My life is so weird.

Then I remember what happened between me and said dragon-man last night and decide maybe weird is the wrong word. Hot seems appropriate. Sexy works too. Mind-blowing. Life-altering. I could go on, but my phone beeps, interrupting my reminiscing about what was absolutely the best sex of my life—thus far.

At the sound of my alarm going off, reality slams back into focus, and I groan again, getting reluctantly to my feet.

The dragon grunts unhappily as I leave the warmth of the cocoon he's made for me with his wing.

"I need to get to work," I say apologetically as I hurry to get dressed.

A walk of shame in yesterday's clothes is not what I had in mind for this morning, but here we are. And I can't afford to answer the questions that would come from being late again. Or worse, being seen exiting the basement.

I'm just finishing pulling my shirt down over my head when a throat clears behind me. I whirl to see Aries standing before me, back in his human form. He's even managed to retrieve those sinfully sexy sweatpants and pull them on.

I watch as he approaches me, wishing like hell I'd thought to bring a toothbrush down here.

"Thank you for keeping me safe and warm last night," I say.

Something like pain flashes in his eyes.

"I'll be safe at work," I start, but he snorts.

"You're only safe if I'm near you."

I shiver because, even though I've only known Aries for a short time, I can't help but agree with him. I do feel safer when he's near me.

"Listen, Hoc and the others will be up and about, so you'll have to stay down here for a bit. I can come back when the coast is clear and help you get back upstairs," I say. He starts to interrupt, but I hurry to add, "I think you should check out the passageway you found in my closet today. Everyone who works here will be focused on their duties, so wherever it leads, you should be able to get in and get out without being seen."

He studies me, looking like he's about to argue, but then finally, he nods. "All right, Paige."

Before I can move past him to leave, he grabs me and yanks me toward him, covering my mouth with his. The kiss is passionate. Desperation laced in every delicious slide of his tongue over mine.

Desperate for what, I can't be sure, but I have the sense that Aries is hurting. I want to ask, to find out what it is that could be affecting this man—this powerful dragon—but I keep it to myself. Likely because I'm afraid that the answer will be that he's homesick.

And the idea of sending him home now breaks my heart.

So, I let Aries kiss me to the point of senseless, until nothing matters but his hands on me. His mouth on mine.

Then, he steps back to let me leave, and I have to force myself to put one foot in front of the other even as it takes me further away from what I really want.

Him.

Upstairs, I manage to slip out of the basement access door unseen. I'm just rounding the stacks toward the break room—coffee is all that matters now—when I run smack into a body.

Hoc grunts in surprise, and I jump back, heart thudding.

Trolls don't have the same sense of smell as other supernaturals but still. I do not want him catching a whiff of what—or who—I did last night.

"Hoc!"

"Paige, are you in a hurry?" His brows lift in dry amusement.

"Coffee," I explain sheepishly.

"Ah."

I wait for him to ask why I didn't bother getting any coffee in my own apartment. Or why I still haven't done a grocery order. But he doesn't. Instead, he glances past me to something over my shoulder.

He frowns. "Blossom, you're supposed to be in section

five already. Ted and Ned were due to be relieved twenty minutes ago."

I glance back and find Blossom standing near the water creatures section with a to-go mug in her hand. "I live for nothing else, Hoc," she says sarcastically.

"But?" Hoc asks knowingly.

"I need your darling daughter to accompany me. Girl stuff," she adds hastily.

Hoc shakes his head. "Go," he says to me. "We'll catch up later."

I hurry to join Blossom, sending longing looks to her coffee.

"And Paige?" Hoc calls out behind me.

"Yeah?"

"We should do family dinner," he says. "It's been a while, and I've been so busy—we need to catch up."

Shit. "It's okay," I start. "I understand, you've got a lot on your plate—"

"How about tonight?" he asks.

"Tonight?"

"I'll be up around seven. I'll bring some of that wildebeest casserole you liked so much the last time."

"Actually, tonight is—"

He's gone before I can argue.

I turn back to Blossom, who grins knowingly.

"I think Daddy-dearest can smell your boyfriend on you."

"Ugh. Is it that obvious?"

Blossom laughs. "I think people in the next portal can smell it, sweetie."

"Ugh. Just Extricate me now."

"No way, this is too much fun." She links her arm through mine and leads me into the stacks.

"Here." She holds out her coffee.

"Seriously?" I ask, my eyes wide.

"You need it way more than me, honey. Come on."

I take the coffee and sip generously, giving myself a moment to adjust as the caffeine slides through me. Just when I'm beginning to believe I can handle Hoc in my apartment—or knowing about my "boyfriend" as Blossom calls him—she ruins it.

"That weirdo is back again today," she tells me.

I lower the coffee long enough to side-eye her. "What weirdo is that?"

"The creeper. Mr. Morris or whatever." She arches a brow at me as my stomach sinks.

"So what? Make Ned babysit him for once."

"He's asking for you."

"I have to practice for my keeper test," I say.

"Look, no offense, but if you don't know it by now, it's not happening."

"Gee, thanks for the support."

"I mean it, Paige." She pulls me to a stop, facing me. "You've lived your entire life in the Athenaeum. If anyone knows what it takes to be a keeper, it's you. And if the powers that be can't see that, well, they're even bigger asshats than I thought. And that's pretty big because I think they're fucking—"

"Okay, I get it." I glance around, more paranoid than usual.

"I'm just saying. You're going to rock that test."

"Thank you."

"And I was thinking," she says, pulling me along again. "I like your idea."

"Which idea was that?"

"My birthday drinks idea."

"Oh." I nearly trip as I whip my head toward her. "You want to go out with Mag?"

"What? Fuck no. I meant you and me... and your boy toy." She winks. "We should make a night of it. Go to that bar you talked about."

The answering adrenaline rush is like a punch to my gut. "Really?"

I try my best to play it cool, but this is it. This is how I get Aries home.

"Really," she says. "Besides, you're not a full keeper yet, so there's no rule about not being in the same public place together anyway. Oh shit, there he is."

I look up and find Morris directly above us in the alchemy section. He's seated at one of the research tables, bent over a book.

I hesitate.

Impossibly, he chooses that moment to look away from his book—and directly down at me. A shiver goes up my spine. There's something about him. Something that makes the hair on the back of my neck stand on end.

Blossom pulls her arm free and steps back. "A keeper test is nothing compared to that guy," she mutters. "See you later."

She slips away, and I sigh, climbing the steps to babysit for another day.

Morris isn't at the table anymore by the time I make my way upstairs. Fred, the gnome who was watching him, however, waves at me then rides Kitty over the stacks and out of view.

Freaking gnomes.

Chuckling, I move further into the section, but still cannot find Morris. Confused, I head into the stacks, searching aisle by aisle for where he's gone.

The first few rows are empty, so I make my way toward the back. The lighting is dimmer here, deliberately done to protect the ancient tomes stored along the back wall. The glass surrounding these books is impenetrable by anything other than the library's magic. But at the very end of the row, the normally locked cabinet is hanging wide open.

My senses sharpen. I slow my steps, a sense of discomfort creeping in.

"...Apertum, Aperi, Retego, son of a bitch."

The exclamation at the end jolts me into sudden action. Or maybe it's the familiar alchemical commands coming from someone who has no right to utter them. I round the corner and stop short at the sight of Morris standing in the middle of the aisle with a locked book in his hands.

"How did you get that?" I demand.

"Paige." His shoulders relax as if he's relieved to see me here instead of startled at being caught with a forbidden object.

I stalk toward him and snatch the book out of his hands, noting the symbol on the spine representing which collection it's from. "Where did you get this?" I repeat.

"I found it. There."

"How did you get the lock to open?"

"It was open when I got here."

I don't believe that for a second, though I can't figure out how in the world he managed to do it. My wariness goes from shocked to guarded.

"This is one from the Vetus collection. It's not available to anyone but the head librarian."

As I say the words, I shiver. The Vetus collection is ancient and forbidden. Hoc has only ever mentioned these books to me in passing and, even then, only to tell me they can never be allowed to fall into the wrong hands.

"I thought it might hold the answers for what I need."

"Even if it did, it's locked for a reason." I gesture to the mechanism binding the book closed.

"Do you know how to open it?"

I bite back my frustration at the way he's completely disregarding the rules he's broken. "No, like I said, only the head librarian—"

As if on cue, the lock springs free.

I stare down at the book in my hands then up at Morris. He's watching me, but there's no surprise in his expression. Only a gleam of interest I can't quite interpret. My heart begins to pound, a heavy drumming in my ears.

Whirling, I hurry away, clutching the book tight. Now that it's unlocked, it's begun to tremble in my hands. I have no idea what kinds of monsters it holds, but I damn sure don't want to find out either.

"Paige, wait!"

Morris hurries after me. I make it as far as the table and drop the book, holding my hand against the cover so it can't spring open.

"Don't come any closer," I warn him as he comes up beside me. "Clauseruntque," I order the book, but nothing happens. Of course, it won't respond to a normal keeper command. This book is so much older than our current protocols. "Shit."

"Just let it open," the old man urges.

"Are you crazy?" I glance up at him then back down again, gritting my teeth as I struggle to keep the cover closed. Whatever's inside is really shoving against me to get out now. I can't afford to discover what the hell it is.

"Clauseruntque!" I nearly yell the command.

Still, the lock remains free, and the book struggles against my hold.

"Paige, you don't need to worry." Morris's voice is strangely calm, and that, more than anything else, freaks me out. Suddenly, it's crystal clear to me that, whoever he is, he wants this to happen. Maybe even orchestrated it in the first place.

I look over at him, eyes narrowed. "Who are you, and what are you really doing in this library?"

He doesn't answer.

"Tell me the truth," I nearly scream at him.

Behind me, a couple of books fly off the shelf and thud against the carpet. Morris looks from them to me and finally loses his cool as he says,

"I'm just trying to get fucking free!"

His answer shuts me up. I don't understand it, and all I can do is blink at him, still grunting against the weight of whatever's fighting me inside this book.

Morris looks at me like he knows something I don't. When he speaks again, he's calmer, more composed. "Just let go, Paige. Your power is so much bigger than you realize. You'll see. Just let go."

He takes a step toward me, and I panic. "Stop," I tell him, and the force of my voice echoes around us. "Don't come any closer."

"Help me get out, Paige. I know you can do it."

"Get out of what?" I ask, completely confused by this entire sideways fucking scenario.

I still have no idea what's happening here, but one thing is for sure: Morris is definitely a creeper. And his time in this library is officially expired.

"Help me," he repeats, looming closer, and my breath catches. If he attacks me now, I'll have to choose between fighting him off and keeping this damn book shut.

It's not a choice I want to make.

Just before he can reach me, a roar sounds, and a figure drops down from above. Pecs and sinewy muscle flash before me.

A familiar scent slams into me.

Aries.

He plants himself between me and Morris, and I gasp at the sight of him standing here for everyone to see. It's both a disaster and a saving grace. Morris takes one look at the broad-shouldered, shirtless, sweatpants-clad man before him and flees down the stairs and into the central stacks.

Aries starts to follow, and panic unlike I've ever known squeezes my heart until it nearly bursts from my chest. If Hoc finds Aries in this library today...

"Clauseruntque!" I scream the word, more desperate than I've ever been, and the book's lock finally slides back into place. Whatever was struggling to get free is silenced, and the book falls still beneath my hands.

I immediately go after Aries, managing to grab his arm just before he would have hit the stairs. "Wait!"

"He was going to hurt you." His voice is barely more than a growl.

The skin of his bicep turns to scales, and my fear reaches new heights. "Aries." My voice is hard enough to make him turn. "If you go after him, you will be discovered too. And they will take you away from me. Is that what you want?"

His eyes narrow, and the rage radiating from his skin heats it to near-burning. My palm heats, but I force myself not to loosen my grip on him. "I want you to be safe," he says, trembling with the effort of remaining still.

"I am," I assure him.

I let go of his arm and press my hands to his cheeks, forcing his gaze to remain locked on mine. "I am safe," I repeat. "As long as you're with me."

He blinks, and some of the fire in his eyes dims. "As long as I'm with you," he repeats quietly.

"Come on," I say, pulling him into the dark corner of the stacks so I can put the book back where it belongs.

"Where are we going?" he asks as he follows my lead.

"To put this damned book back before it ruins my life. And hopefully, to figure out just what in the hell is going on."

CHAPTER 19
PAIGE

My mind is whirring. Thoughts racing faster than I can even begin to grasp them. At the top of the list? Why the hell was Morris holding a book from the Vetus collection that only Hoc has access to?

Followed closely with: Why the hell was I able to open it—and close it for that matter? Only the head librarian has the power to access that particular section. And for good reason.

"You should have let me rip his spine out," Aries growls as I drag him toward the back of the stacks where I can return this book and we can hopefully get away from here unseen.

"Yeah, because that would be an easy mess to explain." As soon as we reach the open glass cabinet, I stop. We're far enough back that no one will hear us, so I release his hand and fold nearly in half as I suck in a deep breath.

The book remains firmly clutched in my hands, silent now.

"What's wrong?" Aries demands. "Are you hurt?"

"What? No." I straighten again. "How did you even get here? You're supposed to be in the basement, waiting for me to come get you."

He shrugs. "I decided to check on you."

I stare at him. "That doesn't answer my question."

"I can show you the tunnel if you like."

I shake my head, too overwhelmed with what just happened to lecture him right now. "Never mind."

"What's wrong?" Aries asks.

"I'm just trying to figure this out. He shouldn't have been able to even touch this book," I tell Aries.

His brow furrows as he studies the simple leather jacket. "What is so special about it?"

"It's full of ancient spells. Powerful alchemy that predates even the library. The only person in the world who has access to the collection is Hoc." I suck in another breath, and my heart rate begins to slow. "Why the hell does Morris want it?"

"If you'd let me catch the asshole, we could have asked him."

I glare up at Aries. He's clearly pissed that I didn't let him destroy Morris right there for everyone to witness. "Fine. The next time that creepy-ass patron shows up, you can drag him into the shadows and rip him limb from limb. Deal?"

Aries is less than amused. "There shouldn't need to be a next time."

"There you are!"

"Fuck," I mutter as Blossom jogs over. How she found us when we're hidden so far out of sight is unsettling, but at least it's not Morris. Or Hoc.

Aries turns to face her, and the unicorn looks him over appreciatively, gaze lingering on his impressive abs. Jealousy heats my cheeks. He's *my* shirtless dragon. She can get her own.

"You are not supposed to be up here," she says to Aries.

"My apologies."

She turns to me. "Why is he here? Not that he's not fantastic to look at, but Hoc is going to freak even more than when he finds out tall, dark, and delicious here is fucking you senseless every night and visiting you at work every day." Before I can come up with a reasonable response to either accusation, her gaze levels on the book in my hands and darkens. "Why do you have that book?"

"Morris had it," I say as I hand it to her. "He was trying to open it."

"This is from the..." Her eyes land on the symbol and then immediately dart to the open cabinet. "Holy shit. Did he unlock that?"

"I think so," I tell her.

Her gaze turns molten. "That piece of... Where is he now?"

"The wizard ran off," Aries replies. "Paige would not allow me to chase him down."

"Wizard?" Blossom and I both echo.

"That perv isn't a wizard," Blossom says warily. "He's a druid. He told me so."

"My senses don't lie," Aries says simply, and Blossom's eyes narrow as she mulls that one over.

I bite my lip. If he lied about being a wizard, why? And what did he mean about wanting to get free?

"What is it?" Aries asks, and I realize they're both watching me, which means my expression must have given away my concern.

"He told me he wanted my help to get free," I say.

"Free of what?"

"I don't know. He said he wants to get out. He seemed desperate and, for whatever reason, believes I can help him with it."

"He was going to attack you," Aries says in a dangerous tone.

"Well, he's damn sure getting out of this library." Blossom's expression borders on murder, and I have a feeling she intends to do exactly that if she catches up with Morris before he portals home. She nods at Aries. "You need to get him back to your apartment. I need to find Hoc."

"I can find my own way." Aries turns and hoists

himself easily up the towering shelf until he's perched on the top. Above him, the ceiling tiles are already slid aside to reveal the opening he used to come down.

"Don't get caught," Blossom replies. "And while I have no idea how you're getting in and out--"

"The tunnels between floors are—"

She holds up a hand to keep us both from responding. "Nor do I want to know. You'd damn well better leave the library or I'll have to kick your ass. Please don't make me do that."

The corners of Aries' lips twitch in a half smile. "Understood." His dark gaze flicks to me, and my breath catches. "I'll see you back at your place." I nod, understanding what he can't say out loud—that it must be safe to return home tonight, which is at least some good news —and then watch as he hoists himself through the hole in the ceiling and disappears. I watch as the ceiling tile slides back into place like he was never here at all.

The moment Blossom seems satisfied that he actually left, she whirls on me.

"Tell me exactly what happened."

"I came up here and found Morris trying to open that book from the Vetus collection. When he saw me, he freaked and started babbling about me freeing him."

"How'd he get the case open in the first place?" she muses, eyes darting to the glass cabinet again.

"No idea." She looks back at me, and I know what she's thinking.

The only creature remotely powerful enough to do it is a wizard. Which is why wizards are banned from the alchemy section in the first place.

"Did he open it?" she demands. "The book?"

For some reason, I hesitate. "What do you mean?" Blossom is on my side for now, but at the end of the day, she'll always choose herself and her own freedom. Opening a book I shouldn't have the power to open seems like a surefire way to put us on separate teams.

"I heard you yell the incantation to close a book. Did he open it?"

I swallow hard. "Yes."

The lie is vile on my tongue. But she can't know that I somehow managed to open it. Not yet. Not until I understand just how in the hell an intern like me was able to open a powerful book like that. Besides, who's to say it wasn't Morris pulling some trick? A whispered spell or a charm cast before I arrived upstairs? Not that any of his magic should be possible inside the library, but he did manage to open the case, so who's to say he didn't find a way to use magic?

"Shit." Blossom reaches into her pocket and withdraws a small communicator. "Hoc, I need you upstairs in the alchemy section ASAP."

"On my way," he replies, the scratchy sound of his deep voice echoing through my ears.

Panic surges through my veins. "You aren't going to sound the alarm so everyone can search for him?"

She shakes her head. "If he's managed to get his hands on the Vetus collection, protocol dictates I alert only the librarian. This has to be handled delicately."

Delicately. In other words, his fate will be determined by the library itself. And chances are, he's not going to live much longer. I might have been fine with that if it didn't mean getting caught up in the crossfire. And considering I'd been standing beside the guy when it happened, there's a good chance I'll have to answer for this too.

"He didn't read any of it. I caught him just as the book opened."

Her gaze lands on me. "That's good news."

A portal opens just beside us, and Hoc steps through right as it closes. His long robe dusts the floor, his leather shoes peeking out from beneath the hemline. His expression is hard, his brows furrowed in worry. "What is it?"

Blossom hands him the book, and Hoc's eyes widen. "Where did you get this?"

Blossom nods at the unlocked cabinet, and Hoc's expression deepens with worry.

"Paige walked in on Morris trying to open it."

"Morris?" Hoc asks sharply.

"A visitor." She sighs. He's been requesting Paige show him around the last couple of days."

Hoc's gaze darts to me. "How did he get this?"

"I don't know," I tell him honestly. "He already had it when I came upstairs earlier."

"What exactly has this Morris been looking for?"

"He said he was writing an article on ancient alchemy and getting back to the old ways of magic," I say, my voice wavering ever so slightly. "I'm so sorry. This is all my fault."

Hoc reaches out and clasps my shoulder. "It's going to be all right, Paige. You couldn't have known he had nefarious intentions."

"Sir," Blossom says tightly, "you should know that I have reason to believe the visitor might have lied about his origins."

Hoc drops his hand from my shoulder. "What do you mean?"

Blossom hesitates, and my stomach clenches while I wait to see if she'll reveal her source. "He came in as a druid...but new information suggests he might be a wizard."

"I see." Hoc frowns.

I swallow hard, guilt settling on my shoulders like a boulder.

"We will put the library on high alert," Hoc says.

"Do we close the library down?" Blossom asks.

Hoc considers her question then shakes his head. "Not yet. That would only deter him."

"Isn't that the point?" Blossom asks.

"Not quite. If what you say is true, this Morris could be a credible threat. If that's the case, I owe it to the library to pursue him. We want him to come back."

"We do?" I squeak the two words out, hoping I'm not giving too much away with my fear.

Hoc smiles though it's not a friendly one. "We do," he repeats. "Because that's how we're going to catch him." He holds his hand over the cover and whispers, "Semita ipsam Apertio."

Track the opener.

Shit. "Um, exactly how long does this spell take to work?" I ask.

If only they knew the last person to open that book was not Morris but rather the woman standing less than a foot away.

Hoc frowns. "Not long, hopefully." He looks at Blossom. "Call a staff meeting. All available hands. This is a Level Five Priority. When this Morris returns, we want to know he's coming so we can be ready."

"On it."

She and Hoc hurry off, and I watch them go, a lump growing steadily in my gut until it's a full-blown brick. This is not going to end well, I know it.

BY THE TIME I manage to make my way up to my apartment, I'm too exhausted to worry about whether or not some shadow killer waits for me in the hall. After a day of waiting on pins and needles for that damn locator spell to expose me, I am both mentally and physically drained. Not to mention the way I opened and closed that book earlier when I shouldn't be capable.

My mind is so full of questions, and the worst part is that I can't ask Hoc any of them. The one person who might have answers is the same person who I can't let find out about any of it.

The stress leaves me distracted and cranky. In fact, if a shadow killer showed up right now, I'd probably just walk right through his ethereal ass without breaking stride.

Fortunately, I don't have to make that decision, and the hallway is clear, so I let myself into my apartment, still drowning underneath the weight of it all.

Aries is waiting just inside the door, arms crossed. "You're late."

"I had a fucking day," I say wearily. "I'm assuming it's safe to be here, or else you'd be hauling me over your shoulder like a caveman."

"What's a caveman?"

"Ugh. I don't have the energy to fight with you," I warn as I move around and head straight into my bedroom. "I haven't showered in nearly two days, and I spent all damn day worried that the tracker spell Hoc placed on that book was going to track me down and not the asshole it was meant for."

He trails after me. "Why would it track you?"

"I'm showering first." I slam the door behind me and head straight into the bathroom. Honestly? If it wouldn't make more work for me, I would have stepped straight into the shower—clothes and all.

Ten minutes later, I'm stepping out of my bedroom wearing plaid pajama pants and a baggy t-shirt with the words *I believe in Tad Cooper* printed on the front along with a bearded dragon in orange.

My comfort outfit. Perfect for a night of uncomfortable conversations. Because even if I can't tell the others, at least Aries will listen and understand without judging me or worse—punishing me.

"Listen, Aries—" I look up and stop in my tracks as horror and shock war in my stomach in a swirling frenzy.

Hoc stands in my living room beside Aries, a glass baking dish in his hand. He's left his robe behind for once and is instead dressed in khakis and a button-up, which is pretty much his most casual and normal look. But that's where the normalness ends. Because his lips are quirked in a strange smile, his brow arched. And the fact that he's standing here beside my new dragon booty call is the most un-normal thing I've ever seen.

Shitballs.

"Paige." He is only a foot taller than my dragon, which is impressive given he's basically a giant. But right now, I can't be bothered with that fun fact. Not when panic is making me wish Aries would douse me in fire so I could incinerate myself right where I stand. I seriously consider throwing myself into the mysterious stalker passageway in my closet and never coming out again.

When I finally manage to utter real words, what comes out is, "Shit."

Hoc turns to Aries and chuckles. "Humorous, right?"

Aries snorts. "It was."

I glare at him because he's showing no signs at all of worrying about his inevitable death-by-father-figure even though he should be, and then I turn back to Hoc. "I can explain. Hoc, this is—this is my—Aries this is Hoc."

Without waiting for an answer, I move into the kitchen and grab a glass. Then I open a bottle of wine and fill my cup to the brim.

"We've met," Hoc says as he sets the glass dish on my counter. "What I'm more curious about is why you felt the need to hide him from me. I know you're a grown woman, Paige. You could have been open with me about your new friend."

"Ugh." The suggestive way he says '*friend*' makes me cringe. Over Hoc's shoulder, Aries makes a face like he's trying to pretend he's not enjoying this, which only makes it all worse.

I lean closer to Hoc and whisper, "Can we not have the birds and bees conversation?"

Hoc grins. "Wasn't planning on it." He removes the foil covering his infamous wildebeest casserole, and my stomach grumbles traitorously. "Good thing I made plenty. Come on, let's eat." He shoots me a knowing look and gestures to my glass of wine. "Drink up, darling. You'll feel better."

Aries actually snorts at that.

"Do not say a word," I warn him, moving aside when Hoc returns with a serving spoon and goes to work, dishing up the food.

Thankfully, dinner is less murdery than I expect. Aries compliments Hoc on the meal and then the two of them share a friendly conversation about baseball. Which, thanks to his new TV obsession, Aries is able to discuss without alluding to the fact that he'd literally never seen it before a few days ago.

Not once does Hoc ask Aries where he's from or how we met. But neither does he seem suspicious about those things either. By the time we're finished, I've convinced myself that just maybe we've gotten away with this. And for some reason, that thought is what pushes me over the edge. Maybe it's insanity and I've finally snapped, or maybe I'm desperate to have Hoc on my side again so he can give me answers, but either way, I can't let this lie go on.

"I'll handle clean up," Aries offers as he stands and gathers our plates. I don't argue or insist on helping because having a few moments alone with Hoc is what I need to alleviate this weight on my chest.

He's *always* been there for me.

And I've repaid him by lying.

"I need to tell you something," I say when we're alone in the living room.

Hoc turns to me. "I rather like Aries. He seems quite fond of you, too."

"Yeah. He's great. Seriously, Hoc. I need to talk to you."

"And I, you," he replies. Before I can launch into the whole fucked up story, he pins me with an arched brow and a knowing gleam in his eye. "Paige, do you honestly believe anything happens in this library that I don't know about?"

I sit back as if his words are a physical blow. And honestly, they might as well be. My stomach fills with rocks, a pit of dread ready to swallow me whole.

"I know that you released Aries from one of the books," he says softly, keeping his voice low.

I gape at him, too far gone to think about denying it. "What? How?"

Hoc smiles. "My dear daughter, I felt the shift in magic the moment it happened." Shit. Of course he did. He's the head librarian, and this damned place is like a living, breathing stalker. Ugh. "Why did you not come to me?" he adds.

"Are you actually asking me that?" I scoff. "You would have killed him."

Hoc's expression shifts to one of guilt. "Is that what you truly think of me?"

"I know the rules," I say. "Rules you're required to enforce. I know what happened during the Extrication."

He winces at that. "I've made mistakes," he says

softly. "And with those mistakes, I condemned an entire world. Your world." I blink back tears at the thought of my parents, who will never meet Aries. Never know what I've done with my life. How hard I've worked. "After that, I promised myself I would not make the same choice again, which is why I allowed you to handle this situation on your own." His gaze flicks to where Aries stands at the sink, washing our dishes, then back to me. "Had you come to me, though, we would have simply erased his memory and sent him back."

I feel stupid.

Foolish.

My eyes fill with hot tears, so I shift my gaze down. Shame heats my cheeks. Because of my own selfish desire to become a keeper, I put Aries and his entire world at risk.

Who knows what's happened in his world since he's been gone?

But more than the guilt over my own mistake, I feel bad that I don't regret it. Not really. Sending Aries back on that first night would mean missing out on everything that's happened between us since then. How do I tell either of them that I am not sorry after all?

Hoc places his hand over mine, and the warmth makes my shame grow. "I'm sorry," he says softly.

"You're sorry? I released a dragon." I glance over, not at all surprised to see that Aries has stopped washing dishes and turned to face us. He knows now—knows that

I was wrong in my attempt to fix this mess. I can't meet his eyes for fear of the accusation I'll find there.

Hoc sighs. "I'm sorry that you did not feel you could come to me."

I don't know what to say to that—except that, whatever happens to me, I know I can't let Aries be punished for it. I meet Hoc's gaze. "And now? Will you take this to the council? There's no way they're going to let him just walk out of here."

Hoc releases my hand and glances back at Aries. "I see no reason to alert the council. We can merely report it as a quick release and return."

"You would do that?" My heart swells—and also breaks. Sending Aries back...saying goodbye...it's more than I can bear.

"That you even doubt me breaks my heart." He shakes his head sadly.

"I just... I knew how much you wanted me to succeed at this," I tell him. "And then I messed up with the wyvern, and I didn't want to disappoint you anymore."

"The only disappointment I could ever feel would be over losing your trust and confidence." He glances from me to Aries and pushes to his feet. "That goes for you too, son. I hope you know I would do anything to protect Paige, including protecting those she cares about."

"I appreciate that," Aries tells him.

Hoc offers his hand, and Aries shakes it in a friendly

gesture, though it feels more like they're sealing a bond than forging a friendship.

"What about my memory?" I brace myself, not sure I want to know the answer. It probably won't change my decision, but I want to know what I'm facing either way.

"I think we can work something out," he says with a promising smile that makes my heart swell.

"You're really going to send him home?" I ask, trying not to let my own emotions show. Instead, I concentrate on the relief and happiness Aries must be feeling.

"Yes." Hoc looks from me to Aries. "We can do it tomorrow morning," he says, returning his attention to me. "And you're welcome to go with him, daughter, should you so choose."

The breath is stolen from my lungs.

"What?" Aries takes a step toward me, and I can see the hope leap into his dark eyes. I want to ask him about that hope. And whether or not it's for me, for the future Hoc is offering us. Or if he's only thinking of himself and his need to return to his kingdom. But I can't find my voice. I'm too shocked, too worried I've misunderstood or imagined it somehow.

"I can see how you feel about him," Hoc says. "And Aries clearly loves you." I try not to react at the L-word, but heat flares in my cheeks. Hoc goes on like he hasn't just dropped a bomb between us. "If you so choose, child, I will send you with him."

I clear my throat, purposely avoiding Aries' eyes. "But the library—"

"Will find another keeper. Don't give up on your own happiness for this old place. I've spent far too many years doing just that." He stands and smiles, the sadness in his eyes making him look older than his years. "Take tonight to think about it and make your choice. Just know that I support you regardless of what you decide." He wraps his arms around me and pulls me in. "The fact that you tried to solve your problem with no casualties or further damage to the books shows me just what a fantastic librarian you will make one day. Should that be the path you choose." He squeezes me one final time then releases me to shake Aries's hand.

"Thank you," Aries says.

"You're welcome. Thank you for protecting my daughter today."

After ushering Hoc out and closing the door, I turn to Aries. "I'm so sorry, Aries. I should have just gone to him in the first—" I'm silenced when his lips capture mine.

At the contact, all thought leaves my brain. There is only this. Only Aries. And how badly I want him. No, how badly I need him.

His mouth is hard on mine—demanding. I grip his arms as he reaches down and lifts me, pinning me against the door. Heat pulsates through me, a wave that consumes as it spreads.

I should stop this or at least slow it down. We should

talk. Discuss what this could mean. But I don't even know what to say. And in this moment, our bodies are saying it for us. I want him. He wants me. That's all that matters now.

He tears at my shirt, ripping it over my head and capturing my nipple in his mouth. I moan and arch back to give him more access as he continues sucking it between his lips.

He's rough.

Frenzied.

I tear at his shirt, too, not bothering to care that I'm ripping it clean from his body. The fabric flies, and Aries spins us, laying me back against the coffee table we just ate dinner on.

He's between my legs then ripping my sweats down and throwing them to the side before kneeling on the floor and burying his face between my thighs.

I cry out, "Aries!" his name a plea on my lips as he draws my clit into his mouth. His large hands grip my thighs, and he shoves them apart to gain better access.

I grip the thick strands of his hair, holding him to me, and he slips a finger inside of me. The pressure is still new as is the damn near instant release I feel when he caresses the flesh inside of me.

I come—hard—the orgasm ripping through my body. Muscles clench and release, but I don't have time to recover before Aries is lowering himself over me and driving into my body. "Yes!"

He slams into me, drawing out only to fill me again and again.

The muscles in his abdomen bunch and release with every thrust, and it's all I can do to cling to the sides of the table.

A resounding crack fills my apartment, and Aries moves like a blur—lifting and pinning me to the wall as my coffee table collapses.

He doesn't break the rhythm—not even for an instant.

My second release is even more potent than the first. My fingernails dig into the flesh of his arms. He comes, his body going rigid mere moments before every muscle within him relaxes.

Sweat gleams on our skin, and although we're both spent, we remain exactly where we are.

Entwined together.

"I choose you," I whisper, the words slipping out before I can overthink them.

Aries pulls back, and I slide down his body. He cups my cheeks and tips my face up to his. "What did you say?"

I hesitate. Maybe I read it all wrong. Maybe this was meant as a goodbye. He doesn't feel for me what I feel for him.

"Say it again, Paige. I want to hear it." His words are a plea, and when I meet his gaze again, I see it; the hope that flared earlier. Maybe I didn't read it wrong after all.

"I choose you, Aries. If you'll have me, I will go to your world with you." Even as I mean the words I say, a twinge of grief settles in my heart. I've made a life here. With Hoc, Blossom, and Mag. My little candy-loving gnomes.

They're my family.

But when given the choice—it's Aries I cannot live without.

"Of course I'll have you. I will love you until the day I draw my last breath. My queen," he whispers then captures my lips again.

CHAPTER 20

ARIES

I wait until dawn has broken before slipping out of bed and dressing quietly. Paige still sleeps soundly, curled against the space I just vacated, and I ignore the twinge of worry I feel at leaving her alone. I won't be gone long, though. With any luck, I'll be back in time to wake her with my mouth between her legs. The thought makes me move a little faster, impatient to finish this task.

Before I go, I make sure her front door is locked securely. Then I let myself into the dark passageway carved into the back of Paige's closet. My roughly fashioned weapons are already stashed inside; a broom handle broken into two halves and sharpened into pointed ends. It's not the worst weapon I've fought with, but I also have no idea what I'll find at the other end of this tunnel, and I find myself wishing for Leo's company at my back. He'd have a dozen jokes to distract and entertain, sure, but when it came time to fight, he'd be ready for that too.

Soon, I tell myself.

Soon, I can return to Astronia where my biggest worry is the horde camped on our borders and not something sinister lurking in my mate's private chambers. My thoughts drift back to Paige and her agreement to return home with me today. What will she think of Astronia? Will she appreciate the land as much as I do? The rolling hills and crystal rivers? Will she be comfortable in the castle?

I resolve right here and now to build her a library fit for a queen. My father's library doesn't exactly boast the kind of romance stories Paige seems to like. But I can fix that. I will scour our world until I have the type of books that will make her happy.

I shake away the thought and force myself to focus on my task. Work now; focus on what's to come later. After all, we'll have the rest of our lives to focus on our own happily ever after.

The passage smells musty; the opening is narrow enough to unsettle my dragon with the rough-hewn walls scraping at my shoulders as I walk, but I shove aside the discomfort as I feel my way along the tunnel. All that matters now is Paige's safety. And while I intend to get her out of this place—today, if possible—I won't leave

Hoc or the others in danger. Not when I know they matter so much to my mate.

I'll see this through, and then we'll go. Together.

The passageway descends at an angle that steepens sharply then levels out again to offer a winding path downward. I have a sense of being below the library itself and wonder if this will lead to the basement where Paige and I slept the night before last. But the passageway continues on, descending farther down than I think is possible.

After what feels like way too long, the passage opens abruptly, and I step into a cavernous space with walls carved from the earth itself and a ceiling so high I'd need my wings to reach it. The scent of stale air hits me, but more than that, the smell of bodies has me tensing and peering more deeply into the quiet darkness.

My skin pricks with awareness. Somewhere in this room, something breathes.

My dragon's sight works fast, but even that is not enough to make sense of the grainy figures littering the cavern. At least a dozen figures, maybe more, are scattered through the space, each one a different shape and size.

I inhale, trying to pick apart the different scents, but I recognize almost none of them.

Except for one.

I have smelled him before.

My lips pull back in a snarl, but before I can utter the

sound aloud, he speaks. "It took you longer than I expected, dragon king."

His voice is taunting, and I loose a growl that echoes deeply through the cavern.

Across the cavern, on a high ledge, a small fire springs to life, and my eyes zero in on the match light that now illuminates the familiar face of the speaker. He lights a candle and then blows the match out, letting it fall harmlessly to the dirt floor.

He looks up, and our eyes meet. Rage boils my blood.

Morris. The wizard.

"What is it you want?" I demand.

"Sshh." He holds a finger to his lips, eyes gleaming with some secret joke. "You'll wake the children."

He gestures around us, and I tear my eyes off my enemy long enough to glance left and right. With the addition of the firelight, I can finally make them out, and horror slams into me.

"Gods," I breathe.

Whatever I was expecting to find down here, it wasn't this. Creatures of all forms slumber quietly in their respective spaces. Some are smaller, furry, almost docile in sleep. But some are enormous, grotesque, with sharp teeth that glow in the flickering light. Each one is chained to the floor, though, looking at them now, I can't imagine those chains would hold long if they decided they wanted to be free.

"What is this?" I ask quietly.

Morris smiles, a cruel twist of his mouth that says far more than his words do. “My new friends. I’ve been waiting to introduce you.”

“You don’t even know me,” I say.

He laughs, and the sound grates on me. “I know more than you think, your highness. On the other hand, I’m afraid it is you who doesn’t know me.”

“You’re Morris. The wizard.”

Even across this distance, I can see that I’ve offended him. “I am Constantine. And I am so much more than a lowly wizard, beast.”

“From where I stand, you look like nothing more than a thief--of books and creatures.”

“Where you stand is a fragile place,” he warns, gesturing to the sleeping beasts surrounding me. “One word from me, and they’ll end you where you stand.”

My eyes catch on something propped against the rock wall behind him. A book. It’s worn around the edges, though not ornate or important looking like the one Paige showed me earlier. This one is plain and unsuspecting yet clearly important to him, or it wouldn’t be up on that ledge with him instead of down here with his pets.

My gaze snaps back to the man standing above us like some sort of ringmaster. Several things are clear even if I don’t fully understand his reasoning.

“These creatures all came from books.”

“Very good, your highness.” The derision doesn’t bother me. Nor does the fact that he knows who and what

I am. His intentions where it involves Paige, however, do bother me.

"You are going to use them to attack the library. Why?"

"It is not your concern."

Fury flashes through me. "You have carved a tunnel straight into the private chambers of my mate. That is absolutely my concern."

"If I wanted to hurt Paige, I could have done so a thousand times already." He tosses the words out so casually, but I have to bite back the urge to roar my rage across this cavern.

I take a step forward, and the creature closest to me stirs. I wait while it rolls away and settles into sleep again. Then I glare at Constantine.

"What do you want with her?"

"I want what we all want, dragon. Freedom." He spits the word at me. Clearly, I've struck a chord. It reminds me of what he said to Paige yesterday. And then I realize what he means.

"You are trapped here. In the library."

"We are all trapped here. In a world that could be ours for the taking if we could only find our way out of this damned library first. We could rule here. More than kings, we could be gods to these lowly fucking humans. If you weren't so spellbound by the first pussy you came across in this world, you'd recognize the opportunity before you."

"Watch your mouth, old man." I take another step, uncaring who or what I wake. The broom handles quiver beneath my tightening grip, but I don't bother to ease my hold. Let them break. I won't need them when I've shifted into my beast and scorched every last monster in this bloody cavern.

He sighs. "I grow tired of this interruption. *Surgit.*"

His command is punctuated by a sudden gasp. In the flickering light, something large rises from the cavern's floor. Yellow, glowing eyes fasten on me and narrow. The creature is already angry.

Constantine smiles at me, satisfied with what he assumes will be my end.

"You might have been the top of the food chain in your world, dragon, but here, you are nothing. These creatures are the most formidable in all the realms. They will tear you apart for a snack. And then you will be nothing more than a figment of someone's imagination once again." His eyes gleam as the creature on the floor below his feet lowers its head, ready to charge at me.

My skin turns to scales along my back and over my shoulders.

"You are nothing here," Constantine calls out. "And when you are gone, her magic will be mine. Perhaps I will keep her when it's done. Make her my queen. She is so damned powerful it's delicious." He presses the tips of his fingers to his lips and kisses them noisily.

Constantine's words jolt me, but not for long. The

creature charges. Its bellow is loud enough to ring in my ears—and to wake the others. Constantine doesn't even move from his vantage point. Fucker. His confidence will be his downfall in the end.

For now, I focus on the glowing eyes as they charge at me and lose myself to the battle.

The creature is joined by two others. By the time they reach me, I've shifted, knocking them aside as I spread my massive wings. My feet turn to clawed talons, and I shove upward just as teeth lock against my ankle and drag me downward again.

The pain of my flesh giving between their teeth only makes me furious. Rage builds, hot as fire, and my dragon rises to the surface of my awareness. I give myself over to the beast inside me, happy to let it destroy my enemies.

As the three surround me, heat builds in my scaly throat. My dragon mouth opens, and fire pours out of me. All three creatures scream as they succumb to the flames and heat, some of them scrambling out of the way. They don't get far.

But more have already woken. Now, they move toward me with murder in their eyes.

Something manages to sneak up behind me. I feel the prick of its claw or pointed weapon as it attempts to penetrate my scales.

Whirling, I find a snake larger than any land animal I've ever seen. Its fangs drip with poison, and I realize too late the prick I felt is much more dangerous than I'd assumed before.

My dragon falters even as I drive my claw across the snake's throat, severing its head. It falls dead, and I whirl, wading through half a dozen other monsters, spilling blood and spitting fire before the venom finally stops me.

My dragon recedes, and I return to human form, falling to my knees and vomiting as the venom wreaks its havoc.

Gods.

If I die here...

I vomit again, and from above me, Constantine laughs.

The rage builds inside me again. My dragon stirs. Out of reach, thanks to the venom's effects, but through blurry eyes, I spot the broom handles in the dirt nearby.

Fuck it.

I'll fight until I can't stand. And even then.

Not a single one of these fuckers will get their hands —or claws—on Paige. Even if it kills me, I will protect her.

Another creature comes for me. A three-headed dog complete with triple the teeth and more than enough speed to rip a small chunk from my arm.

I grab the handles just in time and shove the pointed end of the wood through two of its brains. The third head responds by howling and then falling dead at my feet.

I vomit again and go back to fighting.

By the time I look back at the ledge, Constantine's

expression has fallen from confident to concerned. He should be. Exhaustion clinging to the edges of my awareness, I continue fighting, pushing farther into the cavern toward the ledge where he waits.

I shove my stake through the heart of some creature who looks like a man but with fangs instead of teeth. The other wounds I've inflicted seem to have no effect but this one—a stake through the heart—finally affects him. He staggers and falls away, a viscous sort of blood oozing from the wound. I don't bother retrieving the stake and, instead, leave him impaled with it.

Hurrying forward, I leap onto a lower rock jutting from the cliff and grunt with the effort. From above, Constantine snarls a curse. I keep climbing, trying like hell not to vomit since it'll only slow me down. Below me, the remaining creatures try to follow. I pause to kick out against the closest one and then climb faster.

When I reach the ledge, there's a sharp bird cry, and something winged dives at me from the air. I manage to shove my last remaining stake through its feather-covered breast, and the creature spirals away until I hear it hit the dirt below me.

Finally, I hoist myself onto the ledge, but Constantine is gone. I swing my gaze around to where I last spotted his book. Also gone.

With a groan, I pull myself to my feet and look for another exit. The rock is solid against the far wall, though, and I find no sign of a door or means of escape.

Turning back to the cavern, I spot a single figure moving slowly through the carnage toward the tunnel.

Forgetting the venom in my veins, I launch myself over the edge, arms spread wide as I call for my dragon. It stirs far too slowly for me to recover, and I manage to partially shift just as I slam into Constantine from behind.

Pain explodes in my body as we both go tumbling over bloodied corpses. Constantine cries out as we skid to a stop, each of us flung in opposite directions, and then, everything is silent.

I have no idea how long I lay there.

When I blink, I can't even be sure I didn't lose consciousness. The thought has me gasping and sitting up so fast my stomach swirls. Arms and legs. No scales. But I'm alive.

My ribs ache so badly that I grit my teeth against the pain of breathing. Forcing myself to stand, I scan the bodies littering the cavern floor.

Constantine is gone.

A sound draws my attention, and I look over to find the book lying open on the floor, its pages fluttering wildly. Suddenly, the cover swings shut with a *snap*, and everything is silent.

I make my way toward it, reading the title printed across the front: Constantine the Great.

Freedom, he'd said. That's what he wanted. It's what he gave all of these creatures by bringing them here. Escaped from their own stories, every single one. With the sole purpose of wreaking havoc on an unsuspecting world.

I have no idea how I managed to send him back, but all that matters is he's gone. Paige is safe. Hissing through the pain, I scoop the book into my arms and hurry back through the passage to find my mate.

CHAPTER 21
PAIGE

There should be a trench in the middle of my living room for how long I've been pacing back and forth.

Aries is gone.

He's not in the library.

Or anywhere in this apartment.

And the passageway in my closet is wide open.

Every time I look at it, my heart thuds heavier against my ribs. Fear is a clawed hand clutching at my throat. Last night, Aries promised me we had a future. This morning, he's decided to take off into some creeper tunnel that leads to who-knows-where and get himself possibly killed before that future can even start.

If he's not back in the next ten seconds, I'm going in after him. And if he's not dead, I'll kill him myself.

A noise makes me turn from where I'm wearing the

path toward my bedroom. I whirl just as a body flies out of the open passageway and crashes to the living room floor. I cry out in surprise then freeze at the sight of a bloodied, naked Aries sprawled out on my floor. Panic races through my veins as I sprint and fall to my knees beside him.

"Aries?"

No answer.

"Aries, you better not be dead, or I'll kill you."

He groans and rolls over so he's face up, and I go limp with relief. Then panic crowds in again as I take in the extensive amount of blood coating his body.

"What the hell happened?" I screech. My hands flutter toward the gashes in his chest, but then I stop, unsure what the hell I can possibly do for him. I'm tempted to rush into the bathroom for the usual hydrogen peroxide and bandage routine, but even I know it won't work.

Not when there's this much blood.

It coats his entire body, and there are so many lacerations on his chest and legs that I can't even tell where the hell it's all coming from.

"Aries," I scream when he doesn't respond.

He cracks open an eye and stares up at me. "How was your morning?"

"You asshole!" Without thinking, I slam my fist into his shoulder, and he groans again. "Shit. Sorry. What happened? Where have you been? You can't leave me like that!"

Aries fumbles around beneath his back then lifts a leather-bound book and offers it to me. My fingers brush the smooth cover as I read the title. *Constantine The Great.*

"Where did you get it?"

"Constantine... is Morris," he manages.

"Holy shit." My eyes widen as I stare down at Aries, who looks way too calm considering his beat-up body. "That asshole was from a book."

Aries nods.

"And these wounds?" I ask, fury building as I think of Morris-slash-Constantine hurting the man I love.

"He brought some friends from their books, too," he says, gesturing to—well—all of him.

"We need to get you to Hoc. He needs to—"

Aries coughs and rolls to the side. He curls in on himself and heaves, bile dripping from his mouth.

And then I see the twin fang marks on his back. Each one the size of a drink coaster, they're oozing black with dark lines of venom snaking up through Aries's blood-slicked skin.

"Oh no." Fear claws at my gut as I stumble to my feet. I grab my phone and tap on Hoc's contact information then, as it rings, rush forward and slam the passageway door closed.

"Paige? I'm ready when you are to—"

"Get up here now. Please. Aries is injured." The words leave my lips on a choked plea.

"On my way."

"Bring Blossom," I add quickly. She may not know exactly where Aries is truly from, but should any of Aries' fight follow him out, there is no one else I'd want with us.

"We're coming."

I throw my phone down then jump to my feet and grab an armful of water bottles from my fridge. Falling to my knees beside him, I open one and pour it over the wound to flush the venom.

He doesn't even react.

"Please don't leave me," I whisper as much for myself as for him.

Less than two minutes later, Hoc is shoving my front door open and rushing inside. Behind him, Blossom's blade is out, and she scours the room as the man who raised me falls to his knees beside Aries.

"What happened?" Hoc asks.

"Some kind of fight." I dump another bottle over his injury. The water flushes the wound, but the black continues seeping out. And in.

Please don't leave me.

"Here?" Blossom looks around at my tidy apartment dubiously.

I nod at the closed closet. "There."

Blossom stares at me like I've lost it. Finally, she traipses over and pulls the closet door open. When she sees the passageway yawning at her from the back wall, her eyes widen. She looks back at me incredulously. "What the fuck is this, Paige? Narnia?"

"Not even close."

"Who the hell carved this tunnel into your wall?" Blossom demands.

"Morris," I say grimly. Both their heads whip up to stare at me.

"The one who tried absconding with the Vetus collection?" Hoc asks.

"Yes, but I don't think he was alone. Aries said something about Morris bringing some friends he extracted from books before he passed out. He gave me this." I offer Hoc the book.

"His real name is apparently Constantine. This is his book."

Hoc's eyes flash with rage as he reads the title then hands the book to Blossom. Understanding flashes, and her mouth thins. "I'm going to see what's in there."

"Wait!" Hoc's order rings out sharply, and Blossom stops, looking at him impatiently. I glance back down again as Hoc eyes the injuries on Aries's back. "Son of a bitch."

"What is it?" I demand as Blossom finally walks over to peer down at Aries. Her breath hisses out.

"Basilisk venom," Blossom answers. "Shit."

"Get the antidote. In the cabinet in my office," Hoc orders.

"On it." Blossom turns and sprints from the room.

"Basilisk? As in giant fucking snake? Shit. What is

going to happen to him, Hoc? What's going to happen to Aries?"

Hoc grips my cheeks and holds my face steady. "Listen to me, Paige. Everything is going to be fine. You have vodka here?"

I nod.

"Go and get it. And clean rags."

I push up to my feet on shaky legs and sprint into my kitchen. After grabbing the bottle of vodka from above my fridge and retrieving two clean kitchen towels, I return to his side.

"Sit where he can see you, and keep your hand on his shoulder."

I do as Hoc says and move around to kneel beside Aries. He's so pale. So lifeless. And I cannot help but feel him slipping away from me. "Please don't go," I whisper.

He jerks as Hoc pours the vodka on his wounds. "The water is likely the only reason he is still breathing. You did good."

Blossom rushes through the door, Mag at her side this time. She tosses a container of salve at Hoc, who catches it easily. "The gnomes are holding down the fort downstairs and they're waking Bingo to search for Morris," she says.

"Where was he attacked?" Mag demands. The fact that he doesn't ask who Aries is makes me wonder what Blossom told him on the way up. But there's no time to worry about that now.

"There's a secret passageway in my front closet," I tell him.

Mag marches over to see for himself. He takes one look at the gaping tunnel and mutters a string of curses that, even for him, are impressive.

He glances over his shoulder at me then Hoc. "You got this?" he asks.

"I'm doing what I can," Hoc says tightly. He doesn't look up from his work as he adds, "both of you, go see what you can find, and report back."

Blossom steps up beside Mag, and they share a look. Then the two of them disappear into the dark tunnel.

Their footsteps echo then vanish, plunging the room into silence. I watch as Hoc works, silently pleading with whatever gods Aries comes from to please keep him alive.

"There." Hoc puts the lid on the salve and then manages to lift Aries well enough to get him to my couch. "It's a good thing I'm part troll," he comments as he deposits his cargo and exhales. "Because that is a solid dragon you have there."

I kneel on the floor and grip Aries's hand, holding it tightly in mine as I try to process.

"Paige, he'll be okay now. The antidote works quickly. Trust me," he says. "I've been there."

"Would he have died?" I demand, looking up through tear-filled eyes.

Hoc swallows hard. "Yes."

I close my eyes and suck in a breath. He could have

died. Would have if it weren't for Hoc. "I'm going to kill Constantine."

We both look down at the book still lying discarded on the floor. Hoc doubles back to retrieve it. "It's unfathomable that he was able to escape his book with no one knowing. Even I was unaware of his presence. I'm not sure how that's possible."

Aries stirs then. It's only a breath, but it's enough to bring tears of relief to my eyes. I tighten my grip on his hand then reach out with my free palm and run it over his cheeks as he opens his eyes. "Paige," he whispers.

"I'm okay." He tries to move, but I press him back against the cushions. "Don't worry; Blossom and Mag went into the tunnel to look for Constantine.

"No need," he grunts. "I took care of it."

"Yeah, we should talk about your need to rush alone into so much danger," I say, my tone edging toward annoyed. Now that he's going to live, I can afford to be truly pissed about him risking himself like that.

"We needed to know who put that tunnel here," he says. "And I needed to be sure your family would be safe."

His meaning hits me then, and I have to blink back more tears. Even knowing I was going to leave with him, he still went to check on a possible threat against the people I would leave behind. "Aries... You almost died."

"The library is safe," he says. Before I can argue with him further, he glances past me to Hoc. "You should consider upping your security though. Constantine freed all manner of creatures and locked them in a cavern beneath the library. I can't be sure I got them all."

"There will be a complete inquiry and overhaul, believe me." Now that the urgency is passing, Hoc is beginning to look properly dangerous. "But first, we need to hunt down the creature responsible."

"The creatures I found down there are dead. Constantine is back in his book," he says as he tries to move again.

"Best to remain where you are," Hoc says. "If you reopen that basilisk wound, the antidote won't be able to work as efficiently."

"Basilisk?" Aries draws his brows together.

"Big fucking snake," I tell him.

"Oh. That explains it." He closes his eyes and sucks in a breath.

"You saw Constantine return to his book?" Hoc questions.

"The book was open, and then he disappeared, and it closed," Aries says.

I exchange a look with Hoc, afraid to ask if that truly means he's gone. One look at Hoc's expression, and I know he's wondering the same thing.

"We will lock the library down temporarily. At least until we're sure he's gone." Hoc's gaze lifts to my closet where Blossom and Mag vanished. "And we will magically seal that tunnel then ward it so no one and nothing will ever get through it again."

As if on cue, Blossom and Mag step back out into the

living room. Both shake off a layer of dust, and I notice Blossom's boots are stained with blood. Again.

"What did you find?" I ask anxiously.

"A whole lot of guts and dead things." Blossom shudders, which tells me more than her words ever could. "Your boy gave them hell down there," she adds. "That was quite a fucking mess."

"Mag?" I prompt when he doesn't say anything. Instead, he's looking at Aries, a growing amount of suspicion on his hard face.

"Even I'll admit the destruction was impressive. And don't take this the wrong way, mate, but who the fuck are you?" Mag asks Aries.

I look to Aries, who's still trying to sit up despite my advice against it. "This is Aries. He's my—"

"Boyfriend," Hoc finishes with a wink at me.

Blossom's eyes narrow. "How long have you known that damned tunnel was there?" she demands.

"Aries found it and went to check it out," I reply, hoping to avoid the direct answer.

Unfortunately, my friend is too smart for that. "That doesn't answer my question, Paige." She crosses her arms.

"A few days," I admit.

"And you didn't think to alert any damn one of us? Damn, girl. The sex was truly that brain-melting that you weren't concerned with a tunnel directly to hell? You know what? Don't answer that." She shifts her gaze. "It led directly into a fucking cesspool," she tells Hoc. "Which is where that fucker was living from the looks of it." She glares at me. "You should have told me."

"I'm sorry. I—"

"Save it. I don't do apologies. But don't fucking keep shit from me again." Blossom turns to Hoc. "We'll seal it on this side, but I can't find the other entrance. He was getting them in somehow, though."

"Seal it. Set a ward so if he tries to re-open it, we'll catch him."

"He's gone," Aries insists.

"We have to act like he's not, mate," Mag replies. "Keeper protocol. Unless we see him dead or slammed shut, best to assume the worst. For now. Either way, he's not going to get to our girl again."

Aries growls low and deep in his chest, so I tighten my hold on his hand.

Mag grins. "He's a good one, Paige. I approve." He turns to Blossom. "Shall we go seal this bitch up or what?"

CHAPTER 22
PAIGE

My fingers stroke Aries's hair as we lie in my bed. It's been nearly a full day since Mag and Blossom sealed the passageway and repaired my closet wall like the hole had never been there to begin with. Nearly a full day of me watching Aries breathe and stealing moments away to check on the passageway to ensure it remains closed.

It doesn't matter that Hoc put a protection ward around my apartment stronger than anything the keepers are capable of. I still worry. The longer I sit here in silence and think, the more questions I have. It doesn't make sense.

Constantine digging the tunnel. The monsters in the cavern. Attacking Aries. And for what? Why?

Until Aries wakes up, I won't know.

I do know Constantine's book was sealed when Aries

brought it back. Hoc is running tests now to find out whether Constantine is inside it. It's a tricky thing to test without re-opening the book and unleashing the beast yet again.

I should be relieved that it's all over with. The tunnel is closed. The creatures being kept down there are no longer a threat. And I don't have to worry about the Vetus book tracking me down, either, because the first thing Hoc did was redirect a tracking spell from Constantine's own book since it was a "stronger connection" as he put it.

Then there's the fact that I opened the Vetus book in the first place. And closed it. And I still haven't had a single second to ask Hoc how in the hell I was able to do that bit of magic. It's still on my mind, too, but in light of today, it's not quite as pressing.

In fact, all I can think about is how I only just found the man I love and already nearly lost him. Is this what love is? This gut-wrenching fear that the person you've pledged your life to will be ripped away from you?

Because no romance novel I've ever read covers what to do *after* you find your person. Especially when said person is also a dragon who loves rushing toward certain death. And it's only going to get worse when we get to Astronia, considering he's a king there and responsible for an entire country's safety. Just how in the hell am I supposed to keep him alive long enough for us to actually build a life together?

"What are you thinking about?" Aries' voice is groggy with sleep, but it jolts me. I look down at him and smile softly.

"Nothing."

He scowls. "You cannot lie to me, Paige. We are connected. I can feel your fear."

"Fine," I huff. "I'm afraid of losing you."

"You didn't."

"But I damn near did." I sit up and shove the covers aside, ready to fight this out. It's not fair when he's still so weak, but this fear and frustration has to go somewhere.

With a grunt, Aries sits up against the headboard and flips on my lamp. His sculpted body is already flawless again, the physical injuries healed while he slept the day away.

But he's still pale. And the dried blood I couldn't quite wipe clean earlier still glares back at me; a reminder. And try as hard as I might, the image of him bleeding and in pain on my floor, filled with a deadly venom, will never leave me.

I turn to face him, putting distance between us. "You could have died, Aries."

"Yes," he admits. "But I didn't," he repeats.

"Why the hell did you go down there alone? Why didn't you wake me?"

"What good would it have done? I would have still gone alone, and you would have still been here when I returned."

He's right, of course. Even if I had insisted on going with him, it would have likely gotten me killed in that cavern.

"I don't know," I huff. "But I could have gotten help when you weren't back soon." Tears roll down my cheeks. "I'm sorry. I thought I'd have it more together than this by now. I should have it together." I wipe my eyes with the tips of my fingers. "You're the one who got hurt."

Aries reaches for me, and I go to him, letting him pull me against his chest and cradle me close. It reminds me of the night we spent in the basement when his dragon curled me in safely among its scales so I could sleep. In this moment, I know Aries will always protect me. Even if it means putting himself in danger. "I am alive, Paige. And Constantine is gone."

His tone is final. But I can't help arguing. "What if—"

"He's gone," Aries says as he eases me back and reaches over to cup my cheeks. "You're safe. So am I."

I sigh, willing myself to concentrate on that. "You're right. Even Hoc said with the book being sealed, it is unlikely he is still free."

Aries frowns, and this time, there's a shadow darkening his features.

"What?" I ask, fear rising all over again. "Do you not think--"

"We need to talk about Hoc."

"What about him?"

"There's something you need to know before you

continue trusting him. Something I learned in that cavern. About you."

"What about me?"

He hesitates, and somehow, I know, whatever this is, it's not a small thing. "Aries, you can tell me. I can handle it."

"Constantine dug that tunnel to your apartment for a reason."

"I've been wondering about that." I watch him carefully.

"Constantine said he used your magic to extract those creatures from their books and put them in that cavern."

I stare at him, completely speechless. The language makes sense, but the words... what they imply... it can't be. "That's impossible," I manage.

"He used the tunnel to siphon your magic while you slept," Aries says quietly.

I don't answer, too caught up in the memory of opening that Vetus book. Something about it keeps me from arguing.

Aries watches me, but he's not stopping. He's not treating me like I'm breakable. Somehow, that steadies me. I suck in a breath and blink, assembling my thoughts.

"This can't be right," I say. "Maybe he lied to you. If I had magic, I'd know."

He gives me a strange look.

"What?" I demand.

"Paige, your magic was evident the moment I met you."

My eyes narrow, and my heart thuds wildly. "What do you mean?"

"It feels different than anything else I've ever encountered, but my dragon senses magic, and yours was unmistakable. I didn't even realize what it was, at first. It's as though it's muted somehow."

I crawl off the bed and stand, my chest rising and falling with heavy breaths as my heart thuds louder. Heat rises to my neck and face. I don't know why. Or what I feel. Just that this is utterly impossible.

"What kind of magic do you sense?" I hear myself ask.

He shakes his head slowly like he wishes he had a better answer. "I don't know. It's not like anything I've felt before."

"I have magic." I say the words quietly, mostly testing them on my tongue. It sounds strange, but not untrue, and that shocks me more than anything.

Aries waits, watching me.

"If it's true, Hoc will know," I say, starting for the door.

"If it's true, why didn't he already tell you?"

Aries's questions stop me, and all that heat I felt a second ago leaks out, leaving me cold. I turn back to him and see the glint in his eyes—and finally understand what he's waiting on me to figure out.

"This is why you didn't say anything earlier," I realize. "You think Hoc lied to me—all this time?"

"I think you deserve to know the truth," he says carefully.

For some reason, I can't help but defend Hoc. "Hoc has never been anything but good to me. He took me in when my parents died, treated me like his own daughter. He wants me to become head librarian and run this place someday."

"I'm not saying he wasn't there for you," Aries says quietly. "But if this is true, he's holding back for a reason. And since we don't know what that reason is... You're my concern, Paige. Not him. You come first for me. Always."

My heart softens, and his words take some of the panic out of me. I drift back to the bed and sit, covering my hand in his. "You come first for me, too," I say. "Always."

"I understand if you need to stay here for a while longer," he begins.

"What?"

"Returning to my home with me would take you away from the one person who might have answers. I understand that."

"No, that's not—Aries, look at me."

He lifts his lowered gaze to mine, and I let his dark eyes steady me. One look at him, and I know exactly what I want. What I need. "Look, if I have magic, and no one told me, that means I can't trust them to give me the truth now. I deserve to know what I am, and... if Hoc has been hiding it, I don't think I want to stay here anymore anyway. I need to figure this out, but it doesn't change how I feel about you. Nothing will ever change that." He leans toward me, so I add, "But I will ask him about this before we leave."

He nods. "Of course. We should give him a chance to—"

"I will speak to him alone."

He straightens, eyes blazing. "Absolutely not. It's too dangerous."

My brow arches. "Oh, you mean like it was too dangerous for you to go into that tunnel alone?"

He scowls. "It's not the same."

"Exactly. That tunnel and Hoc are not the same at all. Hoc would never hurt me, Aries. Even if he's lying, he loves me."

But even as I say the words, my stomach churns. Do I really believe that?

"Fine. But I'll be close by," Aries warns. "Close enough to hear. And if he tries anything, I'm coming through the wall."

"Or, you know, you could try the door."

He bares his teeth, and I have to swallow a laugh. The dragon king doesn't scare me. Well, unless you count the fact that I love him so much it's scary.

"You don't scare me, Your Highness," I tease.

Before I see it coming, he grabs my wrist and yanks

me toward him. I nearly sprawl across the bed, but he catches me and pulls me into his arms. His large, muscled, incredibly strong arms. They wrap gently around me so I'm looking up at his scruffy face.

"I love you, Paige Murphy," he says fiercely. "With everything I am."

I meet his gaze, a lump of emotion in my throat as I study his handsome face. For so long, I've wanted this kind of love. Even as I knew it would likely always be out of reach for someone like me.

Then came Aries.

He exploded into my life like the fire-breathing dragon he is, and now, nothing will ever be the same. Shit, if you think about it, a pumpkin spice latte changed the course of my entire life.

"I never want to know what it's like to be without you," I tell him as I cup his cheeks and arch upward to press my lips to his. "I love you, too."

CHAPTER 23

PAIGE

Dressed in grey sweatpants, my biggest T-shirt, and a pair of Hoc's old boots, Aries walks beside me, his large hand enveloping mine as we make our way down into the main part of the library. With his other hand, he carries my bag full of belongings for our trip.

Packing for a far-off land whose fashions and customs are nothing like mine meant a light load to carry. Aries assured me he'll buy me whatever I need when we get there, but it still feels a little strange to be making a permanent move with nothing but a weekender bag. Still, if he can wear the same pair of sweatpants for days on end for me, I can deal with the same for him on the other side of the portal.

As long as we're together, I can deal with anything.

After yesterday's near-death experience, I haven't let him out of my sight. Not that it's been such a chore. We did shower together—safety in numbers and all that.

According to the others, there's been no sign of Constantine, and not a single extracted creature has been discovered within the library's walls. In fact, according to Blossom, the stacks have been extra well-behaved since everything went down in that cavern. I tell myself that means it's all over so I can feel good about leaving the people I love behind today.

The moment we step off the elevator, I smile. Bright balloons and streamers adorn the rows and rows of shelves while a table boasting a *My Little Pony* tablecloth holds a large white cake with red, green, yellow, and blue polka dots.

The gnomes are drinking punch and devouring a pile of donuts—a dangerous combination—though their laughter booms through the space and brings a smile to my face.

Adorable little bastards.

Beneath the table, Kitty waits hopefully for them to drop their crumbs for her. She spots us and watches warily like the anti-social creature she is.

"Uh, what's...?" Aries doesn't finish his question, too busy gawking at where Bingo is lying sprawled on the floor and happily munching loudly on a bone the size of a gnome. His menacing appearance is dimmed only by the pony-print birthday hat someone has strapped to his enormous hound head. A fashion statement the hound doesn't even seem to notice, thanks to the interest in the treat he's devouring. "Is he friendly?"

I laugh. "As long as he has a bone, sure."

Aries doesn't look very relieved.

From where he stands beside the table, Mag looks to me and grins. "What do you think? Too much?"

"My Little Pony? She's going to hate it."

"There's a unicorn on it," he replies as if it's an obvious perfect choice. "I thought she'd feel right at home."

I roll my eyes. "Blossom is going to kill you," I repeat.

"Blossom is going to kill who?" she calls out as she rounds the corner, Hoc at her side. She stops abruptly. Her gaze narrows on the whole setup and décor and then on Mags. "Really?"

He shrugs. "Seemed fitting. Do you like it?"

I expect her to go full Blossom on him—a term I coined after I once saw her rip him a new one for using the wrong font on an inner-library memo. Instead, she simply rolls her eyes again and heads toward the drink table.

I pull away from Aries and make my way over to Blossom, holding out a bag topped with tissue paper. "Happy birthday."

She takes the bag and moves the tissue paper aside,

pulling out the new pair of boots I bought for her. I watch as her eyes give away her excitement, but by the time she places them back in the bag and looks up at me again, she's smoothed her expression over. "Thank you."

"I owed you," I say with a shrug, knowing she won't like it if I make it a big deal.

"I'm still mad at you."

"I know. And I'm sorry."

She glances over at Aries. "Boyfriend, huh? When did he pop the question?"

"Right before he went into the tunnel," I lie. I mean, it's kind of the truth, I guess. It was the night before. If you can consider him asking me to go home with him—forever—as popping the question.

"Then you get a pass on that particular information." She pops a grape into her mouth. "Fine. No longer mad. But no more secrets, Paige."

"Deal." It's another lie, though, and I hate myself for it. Hoc is sending us to Aries's world later, and I'm not allowed to say any goodbyes. No one can know where I've gone.

And as far as anyone but Hoc will know, I simply disappeared. An unsolved mystery. Which works because, once I leave, I can never come back. It's the compromise for not wiping my memory entirely.

Even so, my throat constricts with emotion. I wonder if remembering Blossom but never seeing her again is better or worse than being made to forget her entirely.

"Hey. It's my birthday. You're not allowed to be sad because we fought, so bottle that shit up until tomorrow. Come on, let's eat some cake before the gnomes feed it all to their trash panda." She wraps an arm around my shoulders and guides me over toward the birthday table.

Mag breaks off from his conversation with Aries, smiling at Blossom as we approach. "You're just in time to help me decide on your present," he tells her. "How about a kiss for your birthday? Or would you rather have spankings instead?"

"I suppose that's up to you," Blossom tells him sweetly.

His eyes glitter. "Oh?"

"Sure. Do you want to lose your lips or hand? Your choice." She winks at him, and Aries laughs.

The sound is so carefree, so unburdened, that it catches me off guard. My heart stumbles at the sight of joy on his face, and I realize that this is the first time I've seen such a smile.

Such blinding happiness.

And I decide right here and now that I will do everything possible to keep that smile returning. Starting with making sure Hoc keeps his word to send him home. Though, I guess, after today, it's my home now too.

The party doesn't last long, though it's mostly because Bingo finishes his bone and tries to take a bite out of Kitty. In the ensuing chaos, the tables are upended, and Ted throws up from sugar overload.

After that, Mag and Blossom claim they have to return to patrols, leaving me and Aries with cleanup duty. Aries doesn't complain once, though, and by the time we're done, it's only the two of us left.

If I'm going to confront Hoc, now's the best time. Aries meets my eyes and nods like he's read my thoughts.

"You stay put," I remind him before marching off.

I find Hoc in his office, poring over a large volume lying open on his desk. "Wow, a real party animal," I say. Despite everything I've come here to discuss, there's still this easy bond between us. If I think too hard about that, it'll make me want to weep.

Hoc looks up as I enter and half-smiles. It's a bad attempt, but it's better than nothing. Beyond the mouth-quirk, he looks stressed.

"Did you find out anything?" I ask, sinking into one of the chairs across from his desk. Briefly, I think about the last time I was in here. Hoc lecturing me about "one last shot to become keeper." A role I'm willingly relinquishing which seems ironic considering how far I went to win it.

"Nothing definitive," he says, leaning back and sighing heavily. "And that's what concerns me. Even after all my tests, there's nothing to say he isn't still free."

"But there's nothing to say he is either?"

"The tracking spell I cast on his book is taking more time than I'd like to complete. That could likely mean he's not in this library at all, but it's not confirmed yet," he says. "And until it is, I won't rest."

"I understand. Today isn't exactly the best timing for the party and for..."

He softens. "I'm not going to keep you here, Paige, if that's what you're worried about."

"I understand if you need the extra help," I say, but he waves me off.

"Nonsense. A promise is a promise. Though I will miss seeing you here."

"So will I." My heart aches for what I'm leaving. Blossom. Mag. The gnomes.

"We'll see each other again, though. I can come visit you in your new home," he offers, but I don't answer.

The lump in my throat turns to lead in my gut. "Before I go, I need to ask you something, and I need you to be honest."

"Okay."

"Constantine told Aries..."

"Yes?"

Hoc is watching me so closely, but my thoughts are jumbled. What if he's been lying? What then? But ... what if he doesn't know. I can't leave here—forever—without at least asking for the truth.

"Do I have magic?"

I blurt the words clumsily, but I don't care. At least, they're out. And I don't miss the part where Hoc flinches. Or the fact there's not a single flicker of disbelief or shock at my question.

My stomach drops to my knees.

That's it, then.

"You know," I realize. "You've always known."

"Paige, I..."

He trails off, and I wait, but he doesn't say more. I've never seen him look more lost. For some reason, that pisses me off.

My hands tremble with anger, so I clench them into fists at my sides and remain where I am.

"Hoc, tell me the truth. What am I?"

"Paige, you have to understand; it's much more complicated than you think."

"Maybe I would understand if you'd bothered to share the truth with me. I trusted you, Hoc. You're like a father to me."

The words fly from my mouth like an accusation.

His shoulders sag. "I know. And I tried to tell you so many times, I swear I did."

From outside the door, a growl sounds. It's low, but I recognize it as Aries. He's listening, as promised, and that means he might still come through the wall as promised too. But my emotions are churning, and my thoughts are a heated mess, so I can't bring myself to care.

"What does that mean?" I demand.

Hoc must hear the desperation in my voice because he lifts his gaze to mine and says, "The truth is your magic has the capacity to--"

"Well, well, well, what have we here?"

The voice comes from among the stacks and echoes throughout the library, slicing clean through the tension hanging on Hoc's words. Hoc goes silent as Aries growls for real this time, and icy claws dig into my heart as my chest constricts.

"Looks like you all had a party without me," the voice continues. "My invitation must have gotten lost in the mail."

I race from Hoc's office and stop short at the sight of Constantine. He stands between two shelves, a sinister smile on his face.

Aries is at my side in an instant, Hoc flanking me.

Emerging from opposite ends of the library, Blossom and Mag both draw their swords and move to stand in front of us. I don't know where the gnomes have gone, but I'm praying they aren't far. Something tells me Constantine wouldn't have exposed himself if he didn't have a plan. And whatever that plan is, it can't be good for us.

"What the fuck do you want, old man?" Blossom demands.

He ignores her and looks right at me. Dread coils in my gut, a deadly basilisk prepared to strike at any moment.

"Hey there, fucker," Mag says darkly, waving his sword to get Constantine's attention. "I've been looking forward to meeting you."

"Oh? Can't say the feeling is mutual. See, all of my attention has been on one particular up-and-coming keeper." Constantine grins at me, and bile rises in my throat as I recall what Aries told me. That Constantine has been siphoning my magic away for his own horrific use. Magic I didn't even know I had. "Hello, Paige."

"What the hell do you want?" I clench my hands into fists.

"Your magic. I thought I made that quite clear."

Behind me, Hoc snarls.

"Paige doesn't have any magic." Blossom spins her blade. "But I dare you to try and get to her."

Constantine chuckles at her. "From the moment I saw you, I knew I liked your—what do humans call it? Moxy? It's quite appealing, little unicorn." He stalks closer to the bookshelf and runs his fingers over the spine of one of the books.

It wiggles beneath his touch, and I hold my breath. "Don't," I warn him. So far, no other creatures have shown up, and I can't imagine he'd walk into our midst alone. But if he's truly able to extract, he wouldn't need to arrive with them.

"I'm not the one extracting them," he says pointedly, and my blood runs cold. Aries had said as much, but I hadn't wanted to believe him. Now, the need for answers is so strong that I can't help asking the one person I know I shouldn't trust.

"What kind of magic do I have?" I blurt.

Constantine's eye gleams. He wants me to want his help. And I just played right into his hands. *Dammit.* "Your magic is the most potent thing I've ever tasted," he says. "The stardust of creation itself." His gaze flicks to Hoc, darkening with disapproval. "It's a shame you're not aware of your own potential. Almost as if those around you were jealous, trying to keep you from becoming more powerful than them."

"Everything I've done is to protect Paige," Hoc snarls.

"Your protection has only kept her locked up like a prisoner," Constantine says, eyes flashing. "Though that's clearly what you wanted, isn't it?" Hoc snarls, but Constantine ignores him and looks at me again. "Someone has bound your power, Paige. And I'd wager the troll standing next to you had something to do with that."

I don't answer, but my silence clearly gives away my distrust. Hoc snarls again, this time with Aries joining him.

"If you want, I can unbind your magic," Constantine says.

"Stay the hell away from her," Aries warns.

I look to Blossom and Mag, who are both looking at me with stunned expressions. Their sword points have fallen a bit like they can't quite remember they're supposed to be protecting me.

"And what's in it for you?" I demand of Constantine.

His grin tells me all that I need to know. "Everything,

of course. Nothing's free. Especially not magic, dear. You should at least know that much by now."

He touches the book again, and it vibrates with magic. I inhale a sharp breath. "I won't help you hurt people," I tell him.

His smile vanishes. In his angry eyes, I see the truth: he would never have let me access my full power—not without siphoning it from me and keeping it for himself. For whatever the hell he has planned.

"Put the book down and back away from it slowly," Mag says, apparently recovered from his initial surprise.

Constantine shakes his head. "You should have helped me, Paige. Let me show you the truth. Then I wouldn't have had to destroy everyone you care about." In a blur of movement, he throws the book to the ground, uttering some magical command in a language I don't recognize.

Something jolts through me—a rush of power that catches me off guard—and the cover flies open.

Water sloshes out from between the pages as four huge tentacles explode from inside. Before the creature has fully emerged, Constantine backs away, pulling books off the shelves and unlocking them as he goes. Several more creatures join the first, each one just as deadly—and angry—as the sea monster.

"Get back!" Aries shoves me to the side as he, Hoc, Mag, and Blossom rush forward to engage the creatures.

I duck behind the shelves, keeping an eye on their backs in case Constantine decides to show up.

Sinister laughter to my right has me whirling. Constantine stands at the end of the row, a triumphant grin on his face.

Fiery rage burns through me as I'm hit with another mental image of Aries bloody on the floor of my apartment.

"Come and get me, Paige." Constantine grabs another book. "Before I release every fucking story and rain hell down on your world." He grabs another title and flings it at me. I sprint forward and manage to catch it before it hits the ground and falls open.

He laughs and spins away, sprinting down the hall from me. The same tug from before activates in my stomach, and I gasp, feeling suddenly as if the air has been sucked from my lungs. At the far end of the row, a swirling pool of inky magic flares to life. My feet stumble as my energy is suddenly yanked from my body. The inky magic coalesces into a portal though it's nothing like the ones the keepers can conjure. Through its hazy outer film, I can see what looks like a living room on the other side.

"Paige," Aries bellows.

I turn. His footsteps are heavy as he runs toward me. I wait, unwilling to play Constantine's game. Not when I know it's exactly what he wants. But I don't make it far before magic stops me cold. I struggle against it, but my feet remain frozen where they are. My vision dances as waves of dizziness overtake me.

Aries's eyes widen at the exact moment hands grip me from behind.

I scream as I'm ripped backward and slammed into a hard chest. "Party's over," Constantine growls in my ear. "You're coming home with me."

I wiggle, trying to break free from Constantine. But it's not until something hits me from the side that I'm thrown free of his grasp.

I go down on my hip, air hissing through my teeth at the jolt of pain. But at least I'm free. When I look up, I see Hoc standing where I had been, facing off with Constantine. Both men look murderous now, and Constantine's lips are pulled back in a feral snarl.

His charming façade has been replaced with malice that has me tensing in fear for Hoc. But Hoc doesn't bother attacking. Instead, he whispers a phrase I've come to know well, and magic sparks to life between the two men.

A portal.

This one isn't transparent like the one Constantine tried to conjure, and I have no idea where it might lead. The moment it begins to form, Hoc roars and charges. Constantine tries to jump out of the way, but Hoc grabs him and tries to fling him into the open portal. Constantine grabs Hoc's robes, sending him off balance and unable to step away in time.

They both go stumbling toward the portal opening.

I realize with blinding panic what is about to happen, but there's nothing I can do to stop it. Constantine's grip is too tight; their position too close to the portal for me to reach in time.

Hoc's eyes are wild as he is ripped backward and into a swirling blue light—right alongside Constantine.

"No!" I scream and scramble to my feet, heart pounding.

I run for the man I've always seen as my father, willing to throw myself through the portal if only to save Hoc from being taken in my place, but before I can reach the portal, both Hoc and Constantine vanish through it, and it winks closed.

The others are frozen in shock. The world around me falls completely silent. Not even the books on the ground dare shudder with the threat of opening.

"Paige," Aries calls, but I don't answer him.

Inside me, everything quakes and builds until I can't contain my rage and fear and frustration any longer. The only father I've ever known sacrificed himself to save me. Hoc is gone—and with him, all of the secrets he's kept from me about what I really am.

Unable to contain it any longer, I throw my head back and scream. The shelves around me begin to tremble. Deep in the stacks, thunder booms, and something moans. I ignore it all for the emotion churning inside me like a cyclone.

Aries kneels in front of me, and when my eyes find his, the scream dies in my throat. My chest aches as if the center has been hollowed out.

"Paige, you have to calm down."

I don't know what he means. I've stopped screaming. Then I realize tears are falling in tracks down my cheeks. But I can't stop those. "He's gone."

"Paige," Aries roars.

"I can't—" I close my eyes and take a deep breath, the humming in my ears so damned loud I can hear nothing else.

Something new surges inside of me.

Something that is equal parts terrifying and fascinating.

This is not grief or rage. This is something else entirely.

I shut my eyes, trying like hell to keep my grip on reality while whatever has just woken inside me does its best to convince me to let go.

"Paige," Aries says my name again, and I grasp onto his voice like a lifeline pulling me back to shore.

Slow to the point of pain, I feel myself coming back to the world.

When I open my eyes again, the library is quiet. It's also half-destroyed. Bookshelves lay overturned like dominos. From where I stand in the center, I can now see all the way to the far wall in either direction. Books lay strewn on the ground, and, for a moment, I panic, but none of them shake or shudder with the threat of coming open.

They're still. Too damn still if you ask me. But for now, I'll take it. The destruction terrifies me, but I can't find my voice around the emptiness I feel.

There's a noise behind me, and I whirl, instantly alert.

"Easy," Aries says quietly.

Blossom and Mag stand there, chests heaving with heavy breaths. Their weapons hang limp at their sides—bloodied from battle. But they both look unharmed. They stare at me like they've never seen me before. I want to ask them what the hell has shocked them so badly, but I can't find words.

Eventually, Aries comes around to stand in front of me. He cups my tear-stained cheeks with his roughened hands. "Say something," he pleads.

He looks more worried than I've ever seen. But all I can think about is how Hoc gave himself up for me. Despite the lies. And despite the fight we just had moments ago. He sacrificed himself so that monster couldn't have me.

My wrist burns, and I hiss through clenched teeth as I turn over my arm and note the tattoo that just appeared.

A mark appears that differs from the one Mag and Blossom carry, and it can only mean one thing. The library has lost its head librarian. And in the absence of a sacred protector, it has chosen another.

Me.

Which means I can never leave.

"Paige, please say something," Aries repeats.

So, I do. My heart shatters as I look up at the man I would have walked away from my destiny for. And now, I never can. "He's gone," I choke out. "Hoc is gone. Forever. I belong to this place now."

Keep reading with Dragon Compelled!

FROM THE AUTHORS

Big shout out to Heather's Patreon members for supporting and loving this story before it ever made it to Kindles! Special thanks to Jessica Miller, Ember Nox, Lisette, Kellly McCurdy, Nistily, Anna Blanchard, Deann Fox, Sue Yeates, Rachel Joi Maples, Paula Diaz, Donna Weiss, Kayla Myers, Karen Penn, Samantha Bridges, and Liz Fusselman. I love everything we create together!

And a another big shout out to Jessica's Patreon members! Thank you so much for being a part of the process, and for encouraging me during all of the NSFW art and dirty scenes I tease you with ;)

Thank you Amber B., Jency C., Net B., Deann F., Angela G., Janice, Stephanie H., Paula D., Sissy S., Mercy F., and Sue Y.!

About Jessica Wayne

USA Today bestselling author Jessica Wayne was only seventeen when she wrote her first full-length novel. Titled *One Lovers Ill Will (A book that never saw the light of day.)*, it was at that moment she realized she wanted to be a full-time author.

Life had other plans, though. After spending seven years in the Army, Jessica finally had the time to push forward with that dream.

Now, a wife and mother of three, Jessica spends her days crafting worlds in which anything is possible.

She runs on coffee, and if you ever catch her wearing matching socks, it's probably because she grabbed them in the dark.

She is a believer of dragons, unicorns, and the power of love, so each of her stories contain one of those elements (and in some cases all three).

You can usually find her in her Facebook group, Jessica's Whiskey Thieves, or keep in touch by subscribing to her newsletter via her website: www.jessicawayne.com.

amazon.com/Jessica-Wayne/e/B01MQ1OH4O
tiktok.com/authorjessicawayne
patreon.com/authorjessicawayne
facebook.com/AuthorJessicaWayne
twitter.com/jessmccauthor
instagram.com/authorjessicawayne
bookbub.com/authors/jessica-wayne

About Heather Hildenbrand

Heather Hildenbrand lives in coastal Virginia where she writes paranormal and urban fantasy romance with lots of kissing & killing. Her most frequent hobbies are truck camping with her goldendoodle, talking to her plants, and avoiding killer slugs.

You can find out more about Heather and her books at www.heatherhildenbrand.com, by subscribing to her Newsletter, or joining her Facebook reader group!

Also by Jessica Wayne

Immortal Vices and Virtues World

Welcome to the circus. Enter if you dare.

Slay Me

Protect Me

Fae War Chronicles

Ember is dying.

But as she will soon discover, some fates are worse than death.

Accidental Fae

Cursed Fae

Fire Fae

Vampire Huntress Chronicles

She's spent her entire life eradicating the immortals. Now, she finds herself protecting one.

Witch Hunter: FREE READ

Blood Hunt

Blood Captive

Blood Cure

Rejected Witch Chronicles

She's in love with the man who murdered her. Complicated? You don't know the half of it.

Curse of the Witch

Blood of the Witch

Rise of the Witch

Dark Witch Chronicles

She sacrificed her soul to save those she loves. Now, he must fight to help her get it back, or risk losing her forever.

Blood Magic

Blood Bond

Blood Union

Siren's Blood Chronicles

He's a fae prince in love with a siren.

But they're both too broken to see what's right in front of them.

Rescued by the Fae

Healed by the Fae

Mated by Midnight

Barbarian. Beast. Murderer? One thing's for sure, nothing is as it seems in this crazy town.

Midnight Cursed

Midnight Hunted

Midnight Bound

Accidental Alchemy

My job is to keep the things inside these supernatural books from coming out…unfortunately, I suck at it.

Dragon Unleashed

Shadow Cursed

He can have her body. But never her heart.

Savage Wolf

Fractured Magic

Stolen mate

Blade of Ice

Rise of a Warrior

Fall of an Empire

Birth of a Queen

Cambrexian Realm

The realm's deadliest assassin has met her match.

The Last Ward: FREE READ

Warrior Of Magick

Guardian Of Magick

Shades Of Magick

<u>**Rise of the Phoenix**</u>

Ana has spent her entire life at the clutches of her enemy.

Now, it's time for war.

Birth of the Phoenix

Death of the Phoenix

Vengeance of the Phoenix

Tears of the Phoenix

Rise of the Phoenix

<u>**Tethered**</u>

Sometimes, our dreams do come true. The trouble is, our nightmares can as well.

Tethered Souls

Collateral Damage

For more information, visit www.jessicawayne.com

Also by Heather Hildenbrand

To Hunt A Wolf

To Kiss A Wolf

To Keep A Wolf

Midnight Cursed

Midnight Hunted

Midnight Bound

Wolf Cursed

Wolf Captive

Wolf Chosen

Wolf Revealed

A Witch's Call

A Witch's Destiny

A Witch's Fate

A Witch's Soul

A Witch's Prophecy

A Witch's Hope

Twisted Tides

The Girl Who Cried Werewolf

The Girl Who Cried Captive

The Girl Who Cried War

The Winter Witch

The Spring Witch

A Witch's Heart

Midnight Mate

Goddess Ascending

Goddess Claiming

Goddess Forging

Kiss of Death

Knock Em Dead

Death's Door

Dead to Rights

Dead End

The Girl Who Called The Stars

The Girl Who Ruled The Stars

Alpha Games

Alpha Trials

Alpha Chosen

Dirty Blood

Cold Blood

Blood Bond

Blood Rule

Broken Blood

One Hour: bonus novella

Imitation

Deviation

Generation

Guarded by the Alpha

Alpha Undercover

Mated to the Wilde Bear

The Bear's Fated Mate

Protected By the Bear

The Badge and the Bear

Tragic Ink: A Havenwood Falls story

Contemporary Romance

Risking My Heart

Betting My Heart

O Face

Heather also writes contemporary romcom under the name Moxie Rose. Find out more about her books at moxierosebooks.com.

Quarantine Crush

Corporate Crush

Made in the USA
Columbia, SC
28 May 2023

66ae4b4a-b40b-4b0d-9920-d933f9ebd755R02